We believe a kid who reads is a kid who can succeed.

We believe it's every adult's responsibility to get books into kids' hands and into kids' lives.

We want to make reading fun for kids—through stories and voices that speak to them and expand their world.

We want to make books available to kids—through teacher scholarships, bookstore funding, school library support, and book donations.

We want every kid who finishes a JIMMY Book to say:
"PLEASE GIVE ME ANOTHER BOOK."

Learn more about our initiatives at
JimmyPatterson.org

The **MIDDLE SCHOOL** movie will be

MIDDLE SCHOOL

THE WORST YEARS OF MY LIFE

James Patterson

AND CHRIS TEBBETTS

ILLUSTRATED BY LAURA PARK

JIMMY PATTERSON BOOKS
LITTLE, BROWN AND COMPANY
NEW YORK • BOSTON • LONDON

Copyright © 2016 by James Patterson
Illustrations by Laura Park
Middle School® is a registered trademark of JBP Business, LLC.
Excerpt from *Middle School: Get Me Out of Here!* © 2012 by James Patterson
Illustrations in excerpt from *Middle School: Get Me Out of Here!* by Laura Park
Excerpt from *I Funny* © 2012 by James Patterson
Illustrations in excerpt from *I Funny* by Laura Park

JIMMY Patterson Books / Little, Brown and Company
Hachette Book Group
1290 Avenue of the Americas, New York, NY 10104
JimmyPatterson.org

First Edition: June 2011
Target special media tie-in edition, August 2016

JIMMY Patterson Books is an imprint of Little, Brown and Company, a division of Hachette Book Group. The Little, Brown name and logo are trademarks of Hachette Book Group, Inc. The JIMMY Patterson name and logo are trademarks of JBP Business, LLC.

The publisher is not responsible for websites (or their content) that are not owned by the publisher.

The Hachette Speakers Bureau provides a wide range of authors for speaking events. To find out more, go to hachettespeakersbureau.com or call (866) 376-6591.

Patterson, James, 1947–
Middle school, the worst years of my life / James Patterson and Chris Tebbetts ; illustrated by Laura Park. — 1st ed.
   p. cm.
   Summary: When Rafe Khatchadorian enters middle school, he teams up with his best friend, "Leo the Silent," to create a game to make school more fun by trying to break every rule in the school's code of conduct.
   ISBN 978-0-316-10187-5 (hc) / 978-0-316-10169-1 (pb) / ISBN 978-0-316-27693-1 (media tie-in edition) / ISBN 978-0-316-54647-8 (Target media tie-in edition)
   [1. Behavior—Fiction. 2. Middle schools—Fiction. 3. Schools—Fiction. 4. Emotional problems—Fiction. 5. Family problems—Fiction. 6. Grief—Fiction.] I. Tebbetts, Christopher. II. Park, Laura, 1980– ill. III. Title.
PZ7.P27653Mi 2011
[Fic]—dc22   2010022852

10 9 8 7 6 5 4 3 2 1

RRD-C

Printed in the United States of America

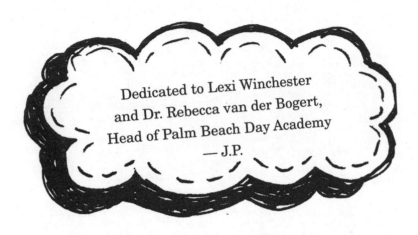

Dedicated to Lexi Winchester
and Dr. Rebecca van der Bogert,
Head of Palm Beach Day Academy
— J.P.

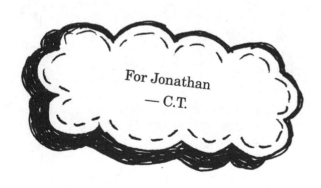

For Jonathan
— C.T.

CHAPTER 1

I'M RAFE KHATCHADORIAN, TRAGIC HERO

It feels as honest as the day is *crummy* that I begin this tale of total desperation and woe with me, my pukey sister, Georgia, and Leonardo the Silent sitting like rotting sardines in the back of a Hills Village Police Department cruiser.

Now, there's a pathetic family portrait you don't want to be a part of, believe me. More on the unfortunate Village Police incident later. I need to work myself up to tell you that disaster story.

So anyway, *ta-da*, here it is, book fans, and all of you in need of AR points at school, the true autobio of my life so far. The dreaded middle school years. If you've ever been a middle schooler, you understand already. If you're not in middle school yet, you'll understand soon enough.

But let's face it: Understanding *me*—I mean, *really* understanding me and my nutty life—isn't so easy. That's why it's so hard for me to find people I can trust. The truth is, I don't know who I can trust. So mostly I don't trust anybody. Except my mom, Jules. (Most of the time, anyway.)

So . . . let's see if I can trust you. First, some background.

That's me, by the way, arriving at "prison"—also known as Hills Village Middle School—in Jules's SUV. The picture credit goes to Leonardo the Silent.

Getting back to the story, though, I *do* trust one other person. That would actually be Leonardo.

Leo is capital *C* Crazy, and capital *O* Off-the-Wall, but he keeps things real.

Here are some other people I don't trust as far as I can throw a truckload of pianos.

There's Ms. Ruthless Donatello, but you can just call her the Dragon Lady. She teaches English and also handles my favorite subject in sixth grade—after-school detention.

Also, Mrs. Ida Stricker, the vice principal. Ida's pretty much in charge of every breath anybody takes at HVMS.

That's Georgia, my super-nosy, super-obnoxious, super-brat sister, whose only

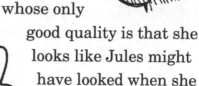

good quality is that she looks like Jules might have looked when she was in fourth grade.

There are more on my list, and we'll get to them eventually. Or maybe not. I'm not exactly sure how this is going to work out. As you can probably tell, this is my first full-length book.

But let's stay on the subject of *us* for a little bit. I kind of want to, but how do I know I can trust you with all my embarrassing personal stuff—like the police car disaster story? What are you like? *Inside*, what are you like?

Are you basically a pretty good, pretty decent person? Says who? Says you? Says your 'rents? Says your sibs?

Okay, in the spirit of a possible friendship between us—and this is a huge big deal for me—here's another true confession.

This is what I *actually* looked like when I got to school that first morning of sixth grade.

We still friends, or are you out of here?

Hey—*don't go*—all right? I kind of like you.

Seriously. You know how to listen, at least. And believe me, I've got quite the story to tell you.

CHAPTER 2

THE MIDDLE SCHOOL/ MAX SECURITY PRISON

Okay, so imagine the day your great-great-grandmother was born. Got it? Now go back another hundred years or so. And then another hundred. That's about when they built Hills Village Middle School. Of course, I think it was a prison for Pilgrims back then, but not too much has changed. Now it's a prison for sixth, seventh, and eighth graders.

I've seen enough movies that I know when you first get to prison, you basically have two choices: (1) pound the living daylights out of someone so that everyone else will think you're insane and stay out of your way, or (2) keep your head down, try to blend in, and don't get on anyone's bad side.

You've already seen what I look like, so you can probably guess which one I chose. As soon as I got to homeroom, I went straight for the back row and sat as far from the teacher's desk as possible.

There was just one problem with that plan, and his name was Miller. Miller the Killer, to be exact. It's impossible to stay off this kid's bad side, because it's the only one he's got.

But I didn't know any of that yet.

"Sitting in the back, huh?" he said.

"Yeah," I told him.

"Are you one of those troublemakers or something?" he said.

I just shrugged. "I don't know. Not really."

"'Cause this is where all the juvies sit," he said, and took a step closer. "In fact, you're in my seat."

"I don't see your name on it," I told him, and I was just starting to think maybe that was the

wrong thing to say when Miller put one of his
XXXL paws around my neck and
started lifting me like a
hundred-pound dumbbell.

I usually like to keep my head attached to my body, so I went ahead and stood up like he wanted me to.

"Let's try that again," he said. "This is my seat. Understand?"

I understood, all right. I'd been in sixth grade for about four and a half minutes, and I already had a fluorescent orange target on my back. So much for blending in.

And don't get me wrong. I'm not a total wimp. Give me a few more chapters, and I'll show you what I'm capable of. In the meantime, though, I decided to move to some other part of the room. Like maybe somewhere a little less hazardous to my health.

But then, when I went to sit down again, Miller called over. "Uh-uh," he said. "That one's mine too."

Can you see where this is going?

By the time our homeroom teacher, Mr. Rourke, rolled in, I was just standing there wondering what it might be like to spend the next nine months without sitting down.

Rourke looked over the top of his glasses at me. "Excuse me, Mr. Khatch . . . Khatch-a . . . Khatch-a-dor—"

"Khatchadorian," I told him.

"Gesundheit!" someone shouted, and the entire class started laughing.

"Quiet!" Mr. Rourke snapped as he checked his attendance book for my name. "And how are you today, Rafe?" he said, smiling like there were cookies on the way.

"Fine, thanks," I answered.

"Do you find our seating uncomfortable?" he asked me.

"Not exactly," I said, because I couldn't really go into details.

"Then SIT. DOWN. NOW!"

Unlike Miller the Killer, Mr. Rourke definitely has two sides, and I'd already met both of them.

Since nobody else was stupid enough to sit right in front of Miller, that was the only seat left in the room.

And because I'm the world's biggest idiot sometimes, I didn't look back when I went to sit in my chair. Which is why I hit the dirt as I went down—all the way down—to the floor.

The good news? Given the way things had started off, I figured middle school could only get better from here.

The bad news? I was wrong about the good news.

CHAPTER 3

AT LEAST I'VE GOT LEO

Do you remember that nursery rhyme about Jack Sprat and his wife? How neither of them ate the same thing, but between the two of them they got the job done? Same deal with me and Leo, except the fat and the lean are words and pictures. Make sense? I do the talking, and Leo takes care of the drawing.

Leo speaks to me sometimes, but that's about it. Conversation just isn't his thing. If Leo wanted to tell you your house was on fire, he'd probably draw you a picture to let you know. The guy is about as talkative as a giraffe. (Oh, I've got a thousand of them, ladies and gentlemen.)

Say hi, Leo.

See what I mean?

Besides, if it's true that a picture's worth a thousand words, then my buddy Leo has more to say than anyone I've ever met. You just have to know how to listen.

Bottom line, Leonardo the Silent is my best friend, at Hills Village or anywhere else. And before his head gets too big to fit through the door, I should say there's not a whole lot of competition for that title. I'm not exactly what you might see in the dictionary when you look up *popular.*

Which brings me to the next thing that happened that day.

CHAPTER 4

RAH, RAH, RAH, YADA, YADA, YADA . . .

After homeroom they'd usually ship us off to first period, but today was "special." There was going to be a Big! School! Assembly! to kick off the year, and everyone was all excited about it.

Of course, by *everyone*, I mean everyone but me.

They herded us all into the gym and sat us down on the bleachers. There was a podium on the floor with a microphone, and a big sign on the wall: WELCOME TO HVMS!!!

The principal, Mr. Dwight, got up and spoke first. After a speech that went something like

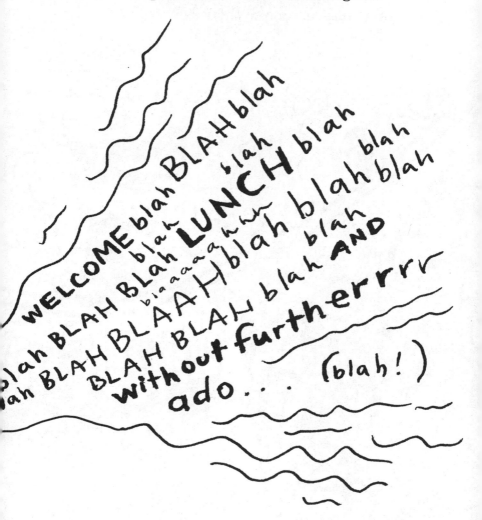

. . . he brought out the cheerleaders, who brought out the football, soccer, and cross-country teams, who brought everyone to their feet, yelling

and screaming. (Of course, by *everyone*, I mean everyone but me.) The only things missing were the circus tent and a couple of dancing elephants.

After that part, Mrs. Stricker announced that anyone who wanted to run for student council representative should come down to the microphone and address the assembly.

Five or six kids from every grade stood up, like they'd been expecting this. I guess Mr. Rourke might have said something about it in homeroom, but I'd been too busy waiting for Miller to drive a pencil through the back of my neck. I hadn't paid attention to too much else.

They started with the sixth graders first. We heard from two bozos who I didn't know, then a guy named Matt Kruschik who ate his own boogers until fourth grade, and then—

"Hi, everyone. I'm Jeanne Galletta."

About half of the sixth grade and even some of the seventh and eighth graders started clapping right away. She must have gone to Millbrook Elementary, because I'd never seen her before. I went to Seagrave Elementary, where we chased rats in gym class, and most of the kids got free lunch, including me.

"I think I'd be a good class representative because I know how to listen," Jeanne said. "And there's nothing more important than that."

I was listening, I was listening.

She was pretty, for sure. She had the kind of face that you just want to stare at for as long as possible. But she also seemed kind of cool, like she didn't think she was better than anyone else. Even if she was.

"I have a lot of good ideas for how to make the school a better place," she goes on. "But first, I want to do one thing."

She leaves the mike and comes over, right in front of where I'm sitting. Then she looks straight at me and says, "Are you Rafe?"

Suddenly, I'm feeling about as talkative as Leo, but I manage to spit out an answer. "That's me," I say.

"Do you want to maybe split a large fries in the cafeteria later?" she asks.

"Sure. I'm buying," I say, because there's a twenty-dollar bill in my pocket that I just found that morning.

"No," she says. "The fries are on me."

Meanwhile, everyone's watching. The band starts playing, the cheerleaders start cheering,

and Miller the Killer chokes to death on a peanut M&M. Then I win the lottery, world peace breaks out everywhere, and Mrs. Stricker tells me that based on my all-around awesomeness, I can just skip sixth grade and come back next year.

RAFE KHATCHADORIAN PLEASE REPORT BACK TO EARTH

"... so I hope you'll vote for me," Jeanne was saying, and everyone started clapping like crazy.

I never even heard most of her speech. But she definitely had my vote.

CHAPTER 5

THOSE OH-SO-CRUEL RULES

The next girl to speak at assembly was Lexi Winchester. I knew Lexi from my old school, and she was a real nice kid. Still, Jeanne Galletta had my vote. Sorry, Lex.

Once the speeches were over, I thought the assembly was done too.

No such luck.

Mrs. Stricker came back to the microphone and held up a little green book so everyone could see it.

"Can anyone tell me what this is?" Stricker said.

"Yeah," Miller the Killer mumbled somewhere behind me. "A complete waste of time."

"This," Mrs. Stricker said, "is the *Hills Village Middle School Code of Conduct*. Everything you need to know about how to behave at school—and how *not* to behave—is right here in this book."

A bunch of teachers came around and started handing out a copy to each student in the gym.

"When you receive yours, open up to page one and follow along with me," Stricker said. Then she started reading . . . really . . . slowly.

" 'Section One: Hills Village Middle School Dress Code . . .' "

When I got my copy, I flipped all the way to the back of the book. There were sixteen sections and twenty-six pages total. In other words, we were going to be lucky to get out of this assembly by Christmas.

" '. . . All students are expected to dress appropriately for an academic environment. No student shall wear clothing of a size more than two beyond his or her normal size. . . .' "

HELP! That's what I was thinking about then. Middle school had just started, and they were already trying to bore us to death. *Please, somebody stop Mrs. Stricker before she kills again!*

Leo took out a pen and started drawing something on the inside of the back cover. Stricker turned to the next page and kept reading.

"'Section Two: Prohibited Items. No student shall bring to school any electronic equipment not intended for class purposes. This includes cell phones, iPods, cameras, laptop computers. . . .'"

The whole thing went on and on.

And on.

And on.

By the time we got to Section 6 ("Grounds for Expulsion"), my brain was turning into guacamole, and I'm pretty sure my ears were bleeding too.

People always talk about how great it is to get older. All I saw were more rules and more adults telling me what I could and couldn't do, in the name of what's "good for me." Yeah, well, asparagus is good for me, but it still makes me want to throw up.

As far as I could tell, this little green book in my hands was just one long list of all the ways I could—and probably would—get into trouble between now and the end of the school year.

Meanwhile, Leo was drawing away like the maniac he is. Every time Stricker mentioned another rule, he scribbled something else on the page in front of him. Finally, he turned it around and showed me what he was working on.

RULES ARE MADE

FOR BREAKING

All I could think when I saw that picture was—I want to be that kid. He looked like he was having a WAY better day than I was.

And that's when I got my idea.

My really stupendous, really, really Big Idea. It came on like a flash flood.

This was the best idea anyone had ever had in the whole history of middle school. In the whole history of ideas! Not only was it going to help me get through the year, I thought, it might also just save my life here at Hills Village.

That was, if I had the nerve to actually try it.

CHAPTER 6

EUREKA!

Did you ever hear the expression "breaking every rule in the book"?

That was it. That was my Big Idea. Break every rule in the book. Literally.

The way I saw it, the *HVMS Code of Conduct* could be my worst enemy here at school, or if I played it right, I could turn it into my best friend.

Sorry, Leo. I mean my second-best friend.

All it would take was a little bit of work . . . and a ton of guts. Maybe two tons.

Leo knew exactly what I was thinking. The idea had come from his picture, after all.

"Go for it," he whispered. "Just pick something out of the book and get started."

"Right now?" I whispered back.

"Why not? What are you waiting for?" he said, and I guess the answer was—two tons of guts.

I just kind of sat there, frozen, so Leo flipped open the book for me and pointed to something on the page without even looking down. When I saw where his finger landed, I almost started having a heart attack.

"I can't do that!" I told him. "What if someone gets hurt?"

"How does this hurt anyone?" Leo said. "Except maybe you."

Somehow that didn't make me feel any better.

"Listen," Leo told me, "you're never going to be one of those people"—he pointed at all the student council candidates and jocks and cheerleaders sitting on chairs that had been set up on the gym floor. "But this," he said, thumping the rule book with his pen, "this is something you can do."

"I don't know," I tried lamely.

"*Or*," Leo said, "you can keep going the way you're going, and every day can be just like this one." He shrugged. "It might not be so bad. There are only a hundred and eighty school days in a year."

That did it. "Okay, okay," I said, and even though

my heart was pounding out "The Star-Spangled Banner," I got up and walked over to where one of the prison guards (I mean, teachers) was standing by the gym door.

"I need a bathroom pass," I told her.

"You can wait," she said.

"'Section Eight'!" Stricker boomed over the microphone. "We're halfway there!"

"Please?" I said, trying to look as much like a pants-wetter as possible.

The teacher gave a big sigh, like she wished she'd been a lawyer instead. "Okay, five minutes," she said.

Five minutes was more than enough. I went out to the hall and into the boys' bathroom while she was still watching me. Then I counted to ten and stuck my head out again.

Nobody was around. As far as I knew, the whole school was inside that gym. It was now or never.

I sprinted up the hall, around the long way behind the office, and then cut down another hallway, through the cafeteria, and into an empty stairwell in the back. By the time I found what I was looking for, I'd been gone only a minute or two.

I stood there, staring at the little red box on the wall.

I could just hear Leo now, like he was right there. *Don't think about it. Just DO it!*

I flipped the latch, opened the wire cage around the alarm box, and put my finger on the little white handle inside. This was what you call the point of no return. My mission, should I choose to accept it . . . and all that.

Still—was I crazy? Was I completely nuts for thinking I could pull this off?

Yes, I told myself. You are.

Okay, I thought. Just checking.

And I pulled the alarm.

CHAPTER 7

CHAOS

I'm not sure what the fire alarm sounded like in the gym, but it was about ten thousand decibels in that stairwell: *wah-AH! wah-AH! wah-AH!* I covered my ears as I sprinted back to the bathroom.

The idea was to make it there before the teachers could get everyone lined up and marching outside. Then I could stroll out like I'd just finished my business and blend into the crowd.

Turns out, I didn't need a plan. By the time I got anywhere near the gym, everyone was already running, walking, and for all I know skipping in every possible direction. I guess Mrs. Stricker hadn't gotten to the part about what to do if a fire alarm sounds (Section 11). In fact, I could still hear her over the mike in the gym.

"Everyone remain calm! Line up with your teachers and proceed in an orderly fashion to the nearest exits."

I'm not sure who she was talking to. It looked like the whole school was already out here in the hall. And in the parking lot. And on the soccer field. And on the basketball courts.

I couldn't believe this was all because of me! I kind of felt guilty about it, but it was kind of . . . amazing. To be honest, only half of that sentence is true. It was more like I knew I *should* feel bad, but I didn't.

Meanwhile, the fire alarm was still blaring—

But it just sounded to me like—

Rafe RULES! Rafe RULES! Rafe RULES!

When I found Leo outside, he gave me a big, double high five. "That's one for execution and one for the idea," he said.

"I can't take all the credit," I told him. "The idea was half yours."

"That's true," he said, and high-fived himself. Then he showed me his drawing again. "Check it out. I made some improvements."

I opened up my copy of the *Code of Conduct* and turned to Section 11, Rule 3: "Students shall not tamper with smoke or fire alarms under any circumstances."

Then I took Leo's pen and drew a line right through it. That felt pretty good too. One rule down and . . . well, all the rest to go.

CHAPTER 8

MY HOME PAGE

On the bus ride home that afternoon, everyone was talking about my little fire drill. It was a rush, sitting there and knowing they were all talking about me.

Of course, everything good has to come to an end. Before long, I was getting off the bus and walking through the front door of my house.

Meet my future stepfather, also known as the low point of my day. His name is Carl, but we call him Bear. Two years ago, he was just this customer at the diner where my mom works. Now, somehow, Mom has a ring on her finger, and Bear lives here with us.

That's Ditka, Bear's lame excuse for a guard

dog. Ditka knows all about "attack" but not so much about "down" or "stop." He usually tries to eat my face for an after-school snack.

"Ditka, down! *Down!*" Bear said, coming out of hibernation as I walked in the door.

Bear pulled Ditka off of me and then flopped back into his Bear-shaped place on the couch. "Hey, Squirt. How was the first day?" (He calls me Squirt. Do I even have to point that out?)

"School was unbelievable," I said. "I kind of, well, sort of, met this amazing girl, and then I set off the fire alarm during an assembly—"

Okay, that's not what I really said, but it wouldn't have mattered if I did. Bear's not exactly a good listener.

"Uh-huh," he said. He reached up and stretched—his workout for the day. "Did you sign up for football yet?"

"Nah," I said. I took a couple of pudding cups out of the fridge and kept moving toward my room.

"Why the heck not?" he yelled after me. "Football's the one thing you're actually good at!"

"Don't worry, I didn't forget I'm a loser, Loser," I said as I zoomed down the hall.

"DID YOU JUST CALL ME A LOSER?" Bear roared back.

"No, I called myself a loser," I said, and slammed my door. "Loser."

Like I said—low point of my day.

Bear and Mom had just gotten engaged that summer, over Fourth of July. That's when Bear moved in. Mom asked Georgia and me what we thought about it before she said yes, but what were we going to tell her? "You're about to get engaged to the world's biggest slug"? I don't think she would have listened, anyway.

Now Mom was working double shifts at the diner all the time just to make enough money, and Bear was spending 99 percent of his time on our couch, except maybe to go to the bathroom or to collect his stupid unemployment check.

Bottom line? My mom was way too good for this guy, but unfortunately neither of them seemed to know it.

CHAPTER 9

CHECK THIS OUT

So, this is what my room looks like. It's the one place at home I can kick back, be by myself, and do whatever I want. Mom says I keep it too messy, but the truth is, I just have too much STUFF.

HELLO

PHONE PILLOW →

→ HOVER BED CONTROLS

net to catch pins →

STRIKE

HOVER BED

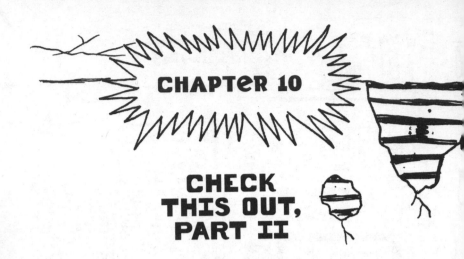

CHAPTER 10

CHECK THIS OUT, PART II

roommate

Okay, I might have been exaggerating a tiny bit there. Really, it's more like this.

(Just kidding. Kind of.)

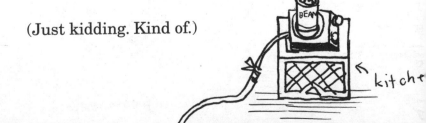

← kitche

GEORGIA ON MY NERVES

About twelve seconds after I slammed my door, Georgia came a-knocking. She knew better than to just barge in. At least I'd trained her that much.

"Enter!" I told her.

She came in and closed the door right behind her. "What's going on? Why was he yelling like that? Are you in trouble?" she said.

In case you're wondering, Georgia is nine and a half years old, in fourth grade, and 100 percent into everyone else's business.

"Go away," I told her. I had work to do. A mission to plan. Besides, since when do I need an excuse to NOT want my sister around?

"Just tell me what he said," she whined.

"Here." I gave her one of my pudding cups. "He said have a pudding cup, okay? Now get out."

She gave me a look that was like, "I'm not stupid, but okay, I'll take the pudding cup," and she didn't ask any more questions.

Mostly, I can't stand Georgia, but I also didn't want her to get stuck in the middle of anything with me and Bear. She was still the kid in the family, after all.

"Rafe?"

"*What?*" I said.

"Thanks for the pudding cup."

"You're welcome. Now close the door—from the other side," I said, and turned my back on her like I expected nothing short of obedience. A few seconds later, I heard her leave.

Finally, some peace and quiet! Now I could get down to work and really figure out where this whole mission thing was going to take me next.

CHAPTER 12

SO THIS IS WHAT MOTIVATION FEELS LIKE!

First of all, it needed a name. I thought about it for a while and came up with Operation R.A.F.E., which stands for:

Rules
Aren't
For
Everyone

I'd be the first kid to ever play Operation R.A.F.E., but not the last. Someday there could be Operation R.A.F.E. video games, Rafe Khatchadorian action figures (okay, so it's not the best action hero name), a movie version (starring me), and a whole amusement park called R.A.F.E. World, with sixteen different roller coasters and no height requirements to ride any of the rides. The whole thing (R.A.F.E. Enterprises) would make me the world's youngest million-billion-trillionaire, or maybe some kind of -aire that doesn't even exist yet. And I'd pay somebody to go to school for me.

R.A.F.E. ENTERPRISES
WORLD HEADQUARTERS

Meanwhile I still had to finish inventing this thing.

I decided that every rule in the *Hills Village Middle School Code of Conduct* should be worth a certain number of points, depending on how hard it was to break. Of course, this meant I could get into some serious trouble, so I decided to make that worth a bunch of points too. And there would be bonuses, for things like getting big laughs, or if Jeanne Galletta saw what I did. Definitely that!

I wrote it all down in a big grid, in one of the spiral notebooks Mom got me for school. (What? This *was* for school.)

That's only part of it. There are a TON more rules in the *Code of Conduct* than that—112 of them, to be exact—but you get the idea.

After I was done writing it all down, I started thinking maybe this whole thing needed some kind of major ending. Like, if Operation R.A.F.E. was going to get me through sixth grade, then I should have something big—no, HUGE—as a kind of final challenge before I could go on to the next level (which was seventh grade).

I'd get Leo to help me, and it would be worth

OPERATION: R.A.F.E.

BEGINNER (no planning, low/no danger)

RULE	≡ POINTS ≡	Witnesses Required?
Talking in class	10,000	4
Running in the hall	10,000	4
Late for class	10,000	4
No Gum	5,000	4
No Electronics	7,500	4

INTERMEDIATE (some planning AND/OR some danger!)

RULE	p-p-p-POINTS!	Witnesses required?
No fighting	25,000	4
Skip class	20,000	4
Break dress code a little	10,000	4
Break dress code A LOT	20,000	4
No bad language/cursing	20,000	4

ADVANCED (major planning AND/OR HIGH danger factor)

RULE	₴POINTS₴	Witnesses required?
Destruction of school property	35,000	(only afterward)
Don't mess with fire alarms	50,000	4 DONE!!
Stealing school property	40,000	

BONUS POINTS Available ↓   ☆ ☆ ☆ ☆ ☆ ☆

FOR What?	POINTS	NOTES
Jeanne G. sees	5,000 - INFINITY	5,000 the 1st time 10,000 the 2nd, etc..
Get big laughs	2,000 - 10,000	depends on # of people
Sent to VP's office	20,000	BEWARE! STRICKER!
Sent to principal's office	30,000	DANGER-DWIGHT!
DETENTION!	50,000	CAUTION- Donatello!
Talking my way out of getting sent to VP's office, principal's office, or detention	100,000	I am the MAN!

half a million points—way more than anything else. It had to be something everyone in school would see, and everyone would remember long after I was gone. But also very high risk. I'd have to *earn* those big points.

I still didn't have any idea how I was going to pull this whole thing off, but it almost didn't matter. I just couldn't wait to start figuring it out. In fact—and please don't tell anyone I said this— for the first time in my life, I was actually looking forward to going back to school.

CHAPTER 13

OFF AND RUNNING

The next morning, Mom set two plates of scrambled eggs in front of me and Georgia and then sat down to watch us eat. She loves to watch us eat, which I totally don't get. I mean, she works at a diner. She watches people eat all day long.

"You were both asleep when I got home last night," she said. "I'm dying to hear about the first day of school. Tell me everything!"

I wanted to say, "Define *everything*," but that would have been like putting up a neon sign that read I HAVE SOMETHING TO HIDE.

The thing is, I don't like to lie to Mom. I mean, I'll do it if I have to, but she has enough to deal with. So instead I shoved half a piece of toast and a bunch of scrambled egg into my mouth and started chewing as slowly as I could.

That meant Georgia went first. Lucky for me, she talks a lot. I mean, a LOT. If Mom hadn't cut her off, I might have gotten all the way out the door without ever saying a word.

"How about you, Rafe?" she asked when Georgia finally took a breath. "What do you think of middle school so far?"

"Well," I said, "it's not as bad as I thought it was going to be."

Like Leo says, not telling the whole truth isn't the same thing as lying.

Mom's eyes got all wide, like I'd just sprouted a second head or something.

"Who are you, and what have you done with my son Rafe?" she asked, joking around.

"I'm not saying I love it —"

"No, but this sounds like a good start," Mom said. "I'm proud of you, honey. You must be doing something right. Whatever it is, just keep doing it."

"Oh, I will," I told her, just before I shoved some more scrambled eggs into my big fat not-quite-lying mouth.

CHAPTER 14

RULES WERE MADE FOR BREAKING

The next few days were just okay. I couldn't top my fire drill from Monday, so I didn't even try. I just stuck to some of the beginner-level stuff to keep things moving along.

On Tuesday, I chewed gum in homeroom, and Mr. Rourke made me spit it out (5,000 points).

On Wednesday, I ran down the hall past the office until Mr. Dwight told me to "put the brakes on there, mister" (10,000 points).

On Thursday, I took a Snickers out in the library, and Mrs. Frurock, who's about 180 years old, told me to put it away (5,000 points). I even took a bite before I did, but she didn't notice (no bonus).

By Friday, I could tell something was missing.

Just breaking the rules by itself wasn't going to cut it. I needed something more. I needed a boost in my game.

I needed . . . (wait for it) . . . *Leo*-izing!

He caught up with me at my locker just before eighth-period English. And of course he knew right away what I should do. Leo always does.

"You're just coasting," he said. "If you're going to play this game, then you need to *really* play it. So I'm going to change things up."

"You?" I said. "Since when do you make the decisions?"

"Since I came up with half the idea for this whole thing," he told me. "Here's the deal. It's two twenty-six. That means forty-nine minutes left in the day. That's how long I'm giving you to earn another thirty thousand points."

"Thirty thousand?" I said. That was more than I'd made in the last three days combined.

"Yep. Otherwise, you lose a life," he said.

"Hang on a second." Leo was going kind of fast, even for Leo. "I have . . . lives?"

"Sure," he said, like it was obvious. "Three of them, to be exact."

"And what happens if —" I didn't want to say it. What happens if I lose all three lives?

"Then you're a big loser, you don't get to finish the game, and the rest of the year will be about as much fun as a case of never-ending diarrhea," he told me.

"Oh," I said. "That's all, huh?"

Leo shrugged. "Gotta keep it interesting."

That's one thing about Leo. He definitely knows how to keep things interesting. I mean, it's not like just because he says something, I have to do it. But what would you rather do—play this game by yourself or with your best friend?

Yeah, I thought so.

"Okay, game on," I told him. I looked up at the clock just as the eighth-period bell started to ring.

"That's forty-eight minutes and counting," Leo said. "Better get busy."

CHAPTER 15

WRITE AND WRONG

I got to Ms. Donatello's English class with forty-seven and a half minutes left in the day. The clock was ticking . . . on my life! (One of them, at least.)

After attendance, Donatello told us that we were going to read parts of *Romeo and Juliet* aloud in class. It was written by Mr. William Shakespeare, who I believe is famous for writing the most boring plays in the history of the universe.

"This is a little advanced," Donatello told us. "But I think you kids are up to it." Obviously, she didn't know the first thing about me.

Allison Prouty, who raises her hand for *everything*, helped give out the scripts while Donatello told us what parts we each had. When she got to me, she said, "Rafe, I think you'd make a fine Paris," and everyone in the room started laughing, right at me.

"Paris?" I asked. "Why do I have to read a girl's part?"

"Paris is a boy," Donatello told me. "He's one of Lord Capulet's best men."

"Yeah, well, he probably still wears tights," I said, but Donatello ignored me.

"Listen to the language as we read through," she told everyone. "Notice how every line has ten syllables. Notice the subtle rhyming. That's not easy to do. Nobody wrote like Shakespeare. Nobody!"

And I thought—*hmmmm*. Idea in progress, please stand by.

"Let's begin," Donatello said. "'Act One, Scene One.'"

It turned out that this Paris guy (he really was a guy) doesn't come in until page 12. That was good. It gave me time to work on my idea. Donatello probably thought I was taking notes like Jeanne Galletta and the other brainiacs, but I was actually hot on the trail of those 30,000 points.

Ten syllables per line? Check!
Rhyming? Check!

By the time we got to my part, there were only a couple of minutes left in class, but I was ready.

"'Act One, Scene Two,'" Donatello read. "'Lord Capulet and Paris enter.'"

Jason Rice was Lord Capulet, and he had the first line. It went something like, "'But Montague is bound as well as I,'" and blah, blah, blah. "'For men so old as we to keep the peace,'" and blah, blah, blah. (I told you it was boring.)

Now it was my turn. I put my paper over the script and looked down like I was reading from the right place. Then, loud and clear, I read, "'Excuse me, sir, there's dog poop on your shoe.'"

"Rafe!" Donatello shouted, but not as loudly as everyone else was laughing, so I kept going.

"'Your wife is ugly, and your daughter too.
I think this play is stupid, so guess what?
I'm out of here and you can kiss my—'"

That's as far as I got before Donatello the Dragon Lady ripped the page right out of my hand.

I knew I was in trouble, but I'll tell you this much: It was totally worth it. Everyone besides Donatello was still laughing, including Jeanne Galletta.

Yes!

And the thing was, nobody was laughing *at* me anymore. Now they were laughing *with* me. That's like the difference between night and day. Or wet and dry.

Or in this case, losing and winning.

CHAPTER 16

THIN ICE IS BETTER THAN NO ICE AT ALL

Donatello didn't have to tell me to stay after class. It kind of went without saying. Once everyone was gone, she gave me a real talking-to.

"What was that about, Rafe?" she asked.

"Nothing," I told her.

"It wasn't 'nothing,'" she said. "First of all, let me say that I noticed you kept Mr. Shakespeare's meter and rhyme in what you wrote—"

"Thanks!" I said.

"—but your behavior was completely unacceptable. There are much better ways to use your creativity, and I think you know it."

I nodded a lot while she talked. It seemed like the right thing to do.

"I'm going to give you a warning this time,"
Donatello said, "but you're skating on very thin ice.
Understood?"

Nod, nod, nod, nod . . .

I didn't hear a whole lot of what she said. All I
could think about was:

No use of foul or inappropriate language at any time	20,000
Bonus: Extra-BIG LAUGHS	10,000
Bonus: Jeanne G. saw	5,000

That was 35,000 points for the day. I'd taken Leo's challenge and blown it out of the water. Even better, I now knew for a fact that Jeanne Galletta knew I existed. That's what you call progress!

As I was leaving, Donatello said, "I hope you've learned a lesson, Rafe."

"Definitely," I told her. "A really good one."

And the lesson was this: There were two ways to play Operation R.A.F.E.—the boring way and Leo's way.

Oh, and I also learned that Leo the Silent is a genius.

NEW RULE

When I got home that afternoon, I went straight to my room with Leo, and we started putting everything that had happened so far into my Operation R.A.F.E. notebook—the rules I'd broken, the points I'd earned, and even some of Leo's pictures, to document the whole thing.

We were just messing around, minding our own business, when I heard Bear start to roar from down the hall.

"WHAT ARE YOU DOING?" he yelled.

Then I heard Georgia. "Nothing," she said. "I just wanted to—"

"I'm watching that! Don't change the channel."

"But you were sleeping!"

"No buts!" he yelled. "You can watch the game with me, or you can get out of here. What's it going to be?" A second later I heard footsteps, and then Georgia's bedroom door slammed.

I *hated* when he yelled at her like that, even more than when he yelled at me. She's just a little kid and he's—well, he's kind of like a little kid too, but the biggest, meanest little kid you ever saw.

"Pick on someone your own size!" I yelled down the hall.

"Mind your own beeswax," Bear said back, and turned up the volume on the TV. It wasn't even worth trying to argue.

"You know what?" Leo said as soon as I closed my door. "We need a new rule."

"I was just thinking the same thing," I said. "Nobody should get hurt from me playing Operation R.A.F.E."

"Especially little kids," Leo added.

And I agreed. I mean, if Miller the Killer accidentally landed in the paper shredder, I wasn't going to cry about it. But otherwise—

"Call it the Don't Be a Bear Rule," Leo said.

"How about just the No-Hurt Rule?" I said.

"Good enough," Leo said, and I wrote that down in the notebook too.

RAFE'S NO-HURT RULE: Nobody gets hurt. All risks are mine, and mine alone. **NO EXCEPTIONS.**

I'm not saying I'm some kind of saint. I'm not even saying this made me a better person, whatever that means. (I'm still trying to figure that one out.) But if putting the No-Hurt Rule into the game could make me even a little bit less like Bear, then I was all for it.

Because Bear was all about hurting.

CHAPTER 18

TEACHERS WANT TO BREAK ME, BUT I DON'T BREAK

You know those vampire stories where the new guy doesn't want to drink anyone's blood . . . until he gets a taste of it? Then all he can think about is blood, blood, BLOOD?

Okay, maybe that's not a good example.

The point is, now that I really knew how to play this game, I was starting to get into it. I spent the next couple of weeks just working on my technique. Leo started giving me bonus points for creativity, and that helped keep me motivated. But Leo wasn't the only one helping.

This might be a good time to introduce you to some of the other people at Hills Village Prison for Middle Schoolers who "motivated" me to be the best I could be at Operation R.A.F.E. Check it out:

These are the cafeteria ladies. I call them Millie, Billie, and Tilly. I think they're part of a

government program to get rid of the middle school population in this country, one lunch at a time.

This is my Spanish teacher, Señor Wasserman.

He's okay as long as you don't make any mistakes,
but if you do—watch out!

Mr. Lattimore is the gym teacher,

and I'm not kidding when I say that nobody ever told him he wasn't in the army anymore.

That last one put me over the top. Mr. Lattimore didn't think the old scooter switch was very funny. (Of course, Lattimore had his sense of humor surgically removed in 1985.) He gave me thirty push-ups, two extra laps, and . . . *ta-da!* . . . my very first detention.

I mean, it's not like I *wanted* detention, but at least now I got something out of it.

I guess you could say I was on a roll. Even when I got home that day, I was lucky. There was a message on the machine from Mrs. Stricker, telling Mom to call the school. That wasn't the lucky part (duh). The lucky part was when I got to it first and accidentally-on-purpose hit the ERASE button.

Mom was at work, Bear was asleep, and Georgia was digging a hole to Australia, for all I knew. As long as nobody had planted any secret cameras around the house (hey, you never know), then I was going to be fine.

CHAPTER 19

APPLE PIE AND CINNAMON

It was a typical Friday night.

Mom wouldn't be home until late, and both Georgia and Bear were asleep by nine—Georgia because she's a kid, and Bear because he's always so tired after a long day of NOT working.

I'm allowed to stay up late on weekends, and since Jeanne Galletta wasn't exactly begging me to go out with her (not yet!), I just hung in and did what I usually do on a Friday night.

First, I took a piece of Swiss cheese out of the fridge. Then I walked over to where Ditka could see me holding it up in the air, but not too close.

"Ditka! Here, boy!"

As soon as he came for it, I ran to the bathroom and threw the cheese inside. I've done this about a million times, but Ditka still falls for it. He pounced on that cheese like it was the last meal on earth, and I just closed the door and walked away. Problem solved.

Next, I went out to the garage and snuck a can of Zoom out of Bear's not-as-much-of-a-secret-as-he-thinks-it-is stash. He keeps cases and cases of it out there, just for himself, but he never notices if a few are missing.

Zoom tastes like chocolate and Coke mixed together, and it has about eight cups of caffeine in every can, which you'd never know, since Bear sleeps so much of the time. I drink mine out of a travel mug, just in case, so he won't see what it is if he wakes up.

After that came the really dangerous part. I tiptoed over to where Bear was sleeping and pried his fingers off the TV remote, one by one. Then I *very carefully* slid the remote out of his hand. It's kind of like defusing a bomb. If it goes wrong, there's a big explosion and everything gets ruined. But if not—sweet! It's the only time I ever get to watch what I want.

I surfed around and found a pretty decent movie, about a guy trying to escape from an island prison by floating away on a raft made out of coconuts. I really wanted to see him do it, but I must have fallen asleep before it was over. Next thing I knew, Mom was waking me up, and there was some kind of infomercial on the TV.

"Rafe, sweetie? Time to go to bed."

I could smell the apple pie and cinnamon on her uniform. She always smells like that when she comes back from the diner. When I'm lucky, she brings some home, and we get to have apple pie for breakfast the next morning.

Mom put an arm around me and walked me back to my room.

"How was your day?" she asked.

"Above average," I told her, which was true.

"You seem different lately," she said. "Happier. It's nice to see."

I didn't know what to say to that, so I just said thanks.

Then she got this look on her face, like when she's trying to figure out what I'm thinking.

"And Rafe? You haven't . . . seen Leo lately, have you?" she asked.

Ouch. I didn't see that one coming.

Leo's kind of a touchy subject in our house. This was the first time in a long time I felt like I had to tell Mom a 100 percent lie, so I just shook my head no. Somehow it seemed better than lying out loud.

Mom looked relieved—which is exactly why I lied, so she wouldn't worry.

"Okay, then," she said. "Remember, if you ever need to talk about anything—"

"I know, Mom. Thanks," I said.

Then she hugged me and kissed me good night, which I was getting kind of old for, but I didn't mind so much. I really like that cinnamon smell.

CHAPTER 20

MILLER THE KILLER RUINS DETENTION DAY

My good luck lasted for another four days, fifteen hours, and (approximately) twenty-two minutes.

It was Wednesday right after school, and I was on the way to my first detention. Everyone else was gone for the day, so the hall was empty, and even though it didn't *seem* like a mistake to stop for a drink of water . . . it was.

I barely got a sip before I felt Miller's XXXL paw on the back of my neck. Suddenly my face was wiping the bottom of that fountain, and I was just trying not to eat the piece of gum someone had left there.

"Well, well," Miller said. "Look who it is."

He pulled me up and slammed my back into the wall. Then he got right up in my face. I could see the Cheetos in his teeth.

"Seems like you're getting a reputation around here," Miller said. "What's your deal, anyway?"

"I don't know what you're talking about," I said.

My heart was going for some kind of world speed record by now. I wanted to just start swinging, but it doesn't take a genius to know that five-six and 150 pounds beats five-one and a hundred pounds every single time. Miller could have turned me inside out before I got off the first punch.

"Listen." He twisted up my shirt in his fist. "You want to prove you're the baddest kid in school?"

"I'm not trying to prove anything," I said.

"Too late," he said, and stepped back. "You and me. Outside. Right now."

"Um . . ."

He held up a finger in my face. "One."

"Ummmm . . ."

Then another finger. "Two."

That's when I remembered—

"I can't!" I said.

"Why not?" Miller said. "Chicken?"

"No. Detention!"

I saw my hole and went for it, right under his arm and up the hall.

"*Detention?*" I heard him say. "This is exactly what I'm talking about. I'm onto you, Khatchadorian! You better watch your back before you *catch-a-door* in the face! You can run —"

I was running, all right, straight to Ms. Donatello's room.

"—but you can't hide!" Miller shouted.

And he was probably right. Unless Hills Village Middle School had a witness protection program, I was dead meat.

Man, I hated Miller.

MORE BAD NEWS

Leo caught up with me before I got to detention. He'd seen everything.

"I've got bad news," he said.

"I just met the bad news," I told him.

"Well, there's more. You also just lost a life. Sorry, bud."

I stopped right there in the hall. "What? No way. What are you talking about?"

"You wussed out on Miller," he said.

"Yeah, well, I didn't feel like donating any blood today."

Leo shrugged. "Could have been worth some good points. 'Section Nine, Rule Eleven: Students will not bully, harass, or fight one another anywhere on school property.'"

"No fair," I said. "Just 'cause I didn't fight him doesn't mean I should lose a life! You never said—"

"I said I'd keep things interesting," Leo told me. "You've got your job, and I've got mine."

"Whatever," I said, and started walking again. "I still didn't lose a life."

"Yeah, you did!" he called after me, and of course I knew he was right.

This was unbelievable. First, Miller nearly turned me into lunch meat, and then Leo took away one of the only three lives I had. Could this day get any worse?

CHAPTER 22

AND TO TOP IT OFF . . .

I thought detention was going to be me, Ms. Donatello, and whoever else had gotten into trouble that week, but when I got to Donatello's room, she was just sitting there by herself.

"You're late," she said.

"Where is everyone?" I said.

"I asked Mrs. Stricker to take the other students for detention today. I was hoping you and I could just talk."

DANGER!

DANGER!

DANGER!

In case you don't already know, when an adult wants to "just talk," it actually means the person wants *you* to talk, all about stuff you don't want to talk about.

In other words, the Dragon Lady had set her trap, and I'd walked right into it.

"Have a seat," she tells me.

"No," I say. "YOU have a seat!" My sword rings in the air as I pull it out of its sheath.

The Dragon Lady's eyes turn yellow. A long stream of fire comes shooting out her nose. I dive over a burning desk, roll, and jump back onto my feet.

Already her tail is whipping out in my direction. Just before it can stab through my ear and into my brain, I clip off the end of it with my sword. Green blood sprays me in the face. She howls in pain.

"Get back!" I yell at her. I can see the fear in those yellow eyes.

But she's faking! She pounces again—wings wide, claws bared, and that razor tail still trying to get inside my head.

The flames are everywhere now. The whole room is on fire, and the heat is intense. I can smell my own skin starting to burn, but I keep swinging. One-two! One-two! One-two! It's getting harder to move, because my sneakers are melting into the floor.

Finally I get her backed into a corner. I raise my sword high, ready to deliver the final death blow—just as her wings open again, and she rises to the ceiling.

She hovers overhead, out of reach of my sword. I swing some more, but it's no good. Of course, her tail can't get me from up there either. I'm starting to think this could go on all night, until—

RIIIIING!

And just like that, my first detention was over.

"I'm disappointed in you, Rafe," Ms. Donatello said. "You have so much potential—"

"I have to catch the bus," I said. "Is it okay if I go?" She just sighed and waved me out of the room.

All students taking the late bus home should proceed to the boarding area now.

I'd survived to be tortured another day, but just like with Miller the Killer, I wasn't sure how much longer I could hold off the Dragon Lady.

CHAPTER 23

WHAT'S THE POINT, ANYWAY?

So what do I get, anyway?" I said.

Leo and I were hanging out in my room, counting up everything I'd done so far.

"Get?" he asked me.

"For all these points. They've got to be worth something, right? What do I win?" I said.

"Depends on how many points you finish with," Leo said. "You need at least a million."

"For what?" I said.

He thought about it for a second. "A week of base jumping at the Grand Canyon, all expenses paid."

"I'll need training," I said.

"No problem. We'll get you the best."

I liked the sound of this. For starters, anyway.

"Then white-water rafting," I said. "All the way down the Colorado."

"And rock climbing, back out of the canyon," Leo said. "Where your Lexus SUV and a fake driver's license are waiting for you."

"Sweet!"

The whole time, Leo was drawing while we talked. Nothing new there—he's always drawing.

"What about Jeanne Galletta?" I said. "Put her in too."

"That's going to be another two hundred
thousand points," Leo said. "But I'll throw in
Bear—you know, so he can get lost in the wild and
adopted by real bears."

This was getting better and better. "In that case,
let him get *eaten* by real bears."

But Leo shook his head. "Nobody gets hurt,
remember? It's already in the notebook."

"I'll make an exception," I told him.

"No exceptions," Leo said. "Besides, you need that No-Hurt Rule. It's the only part of all this that Jeanne Galletta will like."

This is why Leo's a genius. He thinks of everything.

"You know," I said, "you ought to try talking to other people once in a while. They'd like you if you did."

But he didn't answer. Leo the Silent was silent—and that's when I realized someone was outside my door.

"Rafe? Are you in there?" It was Mom.

"Just a second!" I yelled.

Leo did his disappearing act, and I threw my notebook into a drawer just as Mom opened the door anyway. One look at her face and I could tell I was in big trouble.

"No, not in a second," Mom said. "We need to talk—right now!"

CHAPTER 24

I'LL TAKE THE DRAGON LADY OVER THE BEAR ANY DAY

When I came into the living room, Mom was standing there looking mad, just like I expected. But Bear was there too, awake and sitting up. Not expected!

"What's up?" I said, playing it cool for now.

"Did you have detention today?" Mom said.

Uh-oh— busted!

"Well . . . kind of," I said.

"Kind of?" Bear said. *"Kind of?* What does that mean?"

Mom asked him to stay calm, but she kept her eyes on me. "I got a call from Mrs. Stricker. She says she left a message here last week. Do you know anything about that?"

Oh, man—double busted!

Just then Georgia came wandering in, of course. "What's going on? Is Rafe in trouble?" she said.

"Go to your room!" Bear yelled at her.

"Don't talk to her that way," Mom said. "Georgia, honey, this is between Rafe and us. Go on, now."

Georgia disappeared again, but I knew she was just standing in the hall listening where we couldn't see her. At least I'd have witnesses if Bear killed me, which he looked like he wanted to do.

"You're grounded for a week!" he said, standing over me now. "And no more touching the answering machine. You got that?"

"Hang on a minute," Mom said. "I want to hear Rafe's side of this. Carl, sit down. *Please.*" Bear sat, and Mom looked at me again. "Rafe—talk."

Unfortunately, my side of the story wasn't

worth much. I told them all about the scooter in gym class, and detention, and how I'd erased the message on the machine. Even without saying a word about Operation R.A.F.E., I'd still been just as bad as Bear thought I was.

When I was done, Mom took a deep breath.

"Rafe? I'm going to ask you something else now, and I want an honest answer," she said. "Does Leo have anything to do with this?"

I probably would have told her the truth, but Bear decided what he thought about it before I could even open my mouth.

"Again with the Leo thing?" he yelled at me. "I've had it up to here with that! I don't want to ever hear the name Leo in this house again, understand? You . . . freak!"

"YOU'RE THE FREAK!" I shouted back.

"That's enough, both of you!" Mom said, standing up between us. "Rafe, you're grounded until further notice. Carl . . . you go cool off somewhere. I don't want to talk to either one of you right now."

I was already headed back to my room anyway. Our little "talk" was over.

I found Georgia in the hall, no surprise, but I didn't bust her. I just pushed her back toward her own room and then slammed my door behind me as hard as I could.

I wanted to throw something, hit something, and exterminate Bear, all at the same time.

"You know, there are ways of getting back at him," Leo said.

"You shut up!" I told him. "You're not even real!"

I picked up this old ceramic turtle I'd made in second grade and threw it against the wall. It smashed into a million pieces, but I didn't care. I didn't even care about being grounded. It's not like I had two dozen friends waiting to do stuff with me after school every day.

In fact, I had only one friend, and technically he didn't even exist.

"I'm just saying," Leo told me, "I know a way you could get revenge on Bear and maybe even earn some points at the same time. If you're interested."

It took me a while to calm down, but once I thought about it, I realized I definitely was interested.

"Just so you know, this one could really get you into trouble," Leo said.

"Who cares?" I told him. "I'm already in trouble. Keep talking."

CHAPTER 25

TIME OUT . . .

O kay, time out for a second.

I just want to say, it's not like I was trying to hide Leo from you—or at least the part about his not exactly being real.

I know, I know—what kind of sixth grader still has imaginary friends? But I don't really think of him that way. It's just that he's always been around, and there's never been a reason to stop talking to him.

Hmmm . . . maybe I'm not doing too good a job at explaining this.

It's not like I think Leo's really there. It's more like, what if someone *was* there, talking back and helping me figure out stuff? Someone who's always on my side, you know? Like I said before, I'm not exactly popular, so I'll take my help where I can get it. If that makes me weird, or whatever, I guess I can live with that. I hope you can too.

For what it's worth, I've told you way more than I've ever told anyone else (except Leo, of course). You know about Operation R.A.F.E. and my stupid point reward system. You know about my problems with my future stepfarter . . . I mean future stepfather. And, most embarrassing of all, you know about my impossible and very ridiculous crush on Jeanne Galletta.

Here's one more secret, just so you know we're friends: Jeanne Galletta is not going to be my girlfriend by the end of this story. I'm not saying that because I don't have confidence or something. I'm saying it because it's my book and I know how it all turns out. So if you're the type who likes the romantic stuff, and you're waiting around for her to start liking me "like that," I'm just saying— don't hold your breath.

Okay? Now you know all this stuff about me, and I still don't know anything about you. I don't even know if you're still there.

Are you?

And if you are, can I trust you with the rest? I still want to know — are you a good person?

Maybe that's not fair of me to ask, since I haven't even figured out whether I'm a good person or not. I guess you can be the judge.

Here's the deal. If you're okay with me so far, then keep reading. But if you've gotten this far and you think I'm the lowest of the low and I don't deserve to have my own book, then maybe you should stop right now.

Because it only gets worse from here. (Or better, depending on how you look at it.)

Signed, your friend (?),
RK

CHAPTER 26

REVENGE FOR SALE

The next day at school, I put our new plan into
action.

It took until about fourth period for word to get
around. By lunchtime I had a whole line of kids
from every grade waiting at my locker for a nice,
refreshing can of Zoom, right out of Bear's smaller-
than-it-used-to-be, not-such-a-secret-anymore
stash.

Hills Village Middle School is a "sugary drink–
free zone," so something like Zoom is pure gold
around there.

I made it BYOC—Bring Your Own Cup—so
there wouldn't be any marked cans floating
around. One dollar filled the cup of your choice
or emptied the can, whichever came first. Then
I could take the empties home, put them back in

their cases, and wait to see if Bear ever got to the bottom of his stash. (And if he did, I had a plan for that too.)

My customers kept saying how cool this was, and "Thanks, Rafe," including a bunch of people who I didn't even think knew my name. I guess Miller the Killer was right about one thing: I was starting to get a reputation around here.

Business was good too. I'd made sixteen bucks (not to mention 35,000 points) by the time lunch was almost over. I didn't see Jeanne Galletta at the end of the line until she was there at my locker.

Let me say that again—JEANNE GALLETTA WAS AT MY LOCKER!

"Thirsty?" I said, trying to stay cool.

"You know, this is totally against the rules," she said.

"That makes it taste better," I said. (Good line, right?)

Jeanne just looked at me, the same way Mom does sometimes, and even Donatello. It was like she was trying to figure me out.

"Why does it seem like you're always *trying* to get in trouble?" Jeanne said. "I don't get that."

What I did next was probably stupid, but to tell you the truth, I didn't know what else to say.

"Can you keep a secret?" I asked. I took out the *HVMS Code of Conduct* and showed her how I'd already crossed out a bunch of rules.

"Yeah?" Jeanne said. "So what?"

"I'm going to be the first person to break every single one of these," I said. "One rule at a time."

"Oh, great," she said. "Thanks for telling me. Now I could get into trouble too."

"No, you can't," I said. "That's my policy. Whatever happens, I don't let anyone else get hurt. You can even turn me in if you want to."

She just stared at me, but not in a totally bad way. It was more like she hadn't made up her mind yet.

"Go ahead," I said. "Make my day."

Then Jeanne Galletta did something she'd never done before. She smiled right at me. I know this will sound corny, but it was a really, really nice smile. I think Leo was right. She liked that No-Hurt Rule.

Of course, the stupid bell had to ring for fifth period, and that smile disappeared faster than a can of Zoom out of my locker.

"Oh, my gosh, I'm late for science!" Jeanne said.

"Don't worry about it," I said.

"No, that's what *you* do," she told me, and now she was just annoyed. By the time I said bye, she was already going up the hall as fast as she could go without actually running—because, you know, that's against the rules.

"What just happened?" I asked Leo after she was gone.

"I'm not sure about this," he said, "but I think you just got a step closer to Section Four, Rule Seven."

NO KISSING or other public DISPLAYS of AFFECTION are allowed in school!

CHAPTER 27

CRACKING THE
DRESS CODE

When Halloween rolled around, it seemed like the perfect time in the game to take on Section 1, Rule 1: The Hills Village Middle School Dress Code.

Normally this would have been an easy one, but Leo liked it when I upped my game, so he laid down all kinds of challenges and chances for me to earn some extra-big points. Forget the fire alarm. Forget about detention with the Dragon Lady. This was definitely going to be the scariest thing I'd done so far.

The first challenge was just getting out of the house without Mom finding out about it.

"No costume, Rafe?" she said at breakfast.

Georgia was eating a bowl of Cheerios standing up because she couldn't sit down—she was already wearing her big pink wings. I was just wearing jeans and a regular shirt. "Are you already getting too old for Halloween?" Mom asked.

I answered her with one of my not-quite-lies. "It's middle school," I said.

In fact, everything was already in my backpack, and I changed in the bathroom when I got to school—black shoes, black pants, black turtleneck, black ski mask. My backpack was dark blue, but that was close enough. I also had a pocketful of Cheerios for throwing stars, and nunchucks made out of a couple of paper towel rolls with a piece of rope knotted at both ends. It would have been nice to have a sword too, but just try fitting a mop handle in your backpack sometime.

It was only a matter of time before some teacher nabbed me, so Leo said he'd give me 10,000 points for every fifty yards of ground I could cover inside the school. I came tearing out of that bathroom at full speed and just kept running—through the first floor (10,000!), up the stairs (10,000!), down the second-floor hall past the lockers (10,000!),

throwing Cheerios and swinging my nunchucks like crazy.

If there were a highlight reel, the number one play would have to be when I saw Miller the Killer in the hall. I made sure my mask was pulled down tight over my face. Then I took a big windup as I went by, and beaned him upside the head with one of the chucks (10,000!).

"What the—?" Miller turned the wrong way just as I passed him. By the time he'd figured out where I came from and where I was headed, I'd already left him in the dust. He was twice as big as me, but I was twice as fast. Eat it, Miller!

And then—*splam!* I ran right into Mrs. Stricker. Literally.

Let's just say she wasn't in the mood for wrestling.

"What in heaven's name is this?" she said, grabbing me by the arm.

"I'm a ninja," I told her.

"You're a nincompoop," she said. "Take off that mask immediately."

I pulled off the mask.

"Rafe," she said. "I might have guessed. You

absolutely may not run around the school in that costume."

"There's no rule against ninjas," I said. "And believe me, I checked."

"Consider it our newest regulation," Stricker said. "No ninjas allowed, at Halloween or anytime. You're going to have to take that off."

"Okay, okay," I said, like it was a big deal, but this was actually the part I'd been waiting for. Phase two: double points!

I went into the bathroom and came out a minute later without my ninja costume, running just as fast as before.

"RAFE KHATCHADORIAN!" Stricker shouted after me, but I was already gone.

Some kids got out of my way. Some even ran in the other direction. A few of the girls screamed when I came through, but I don't think they meant it. And a few people even yelled stuff like "Go, Rafe, go!" and "Don't let 'em get you!"

Because, like I said, I wasn't wearing my ninja costume anymore. In fact, I wasn't wearing much of anything at all.

Just sneakers, a pair of boxers, and a big old smile.

CHAPTER 28

KICKIN' IT, DUNGEON-STYLE

thought for sure I'd land in Stricker's office for this one. It turned out I wasn't thinking big enough. Ladies and gentlemen, boys and girls, welcome to: THE DUNGEON.

I'm not the only one up for execution today. It's Halloween, after all, so there's a whole dungeon full of people waiting to hear what their torture is going to be.

"Hey," the prisoner next to me whispers. "Aren't you Rafe Khatchadorian?"

I've seen his face before, but I don't know his name.

"That's right," I say.

"I've heard about you," he says. "What did you do this time?"

"I broke the dress code," I tell him. He doesn't look very impressed.

"QUIET!" yells one of the guards. "No talking, under penalty of death!"

I'm getting ready to ask what the difference is, since we're all about to get death sentences anyway, but just then the door to the inner chamber swings open. It's too late for me now. They carry out the body of the last victim, and the Lizard King himself beckons me inside with one long, green, sticky finger.

CHAPTER 29

HIS MAJESTY, THE LIZARD KING

The inner chamber is cold and wet. The Lizard King slides back into his place, across from which I'm supposed to sit. It smells like . . . I don't know *what* in here.

He takes a lid off a jar of something that looks like white jelly beans, and holds it out for me. "Would you like one?" he says.

That's when I see that they're *not* jelly beans, but they *are* moving.

"I'll pass," I say.

He shrugs and pops a couple in his mouth. Something blue runs out over his chin as he chews them.

"It seems you've been making a name for yourself around the kingdom," he says. "My spies tell me you're quite the show-off." When a fly lands on the wall, his tongue shoots out about three feet, and he nabs it. I'm telling you, this guy never stops eating. "Do you have anything to say in your own defense before I pronounce your sentence?" he asks me, around a mouthful of fly.

"I think you're confusing me with my twin brother," I say.

Wrong answer. The Lizard King reaches over and flattens a hand (or is it a foot?) against my face. Either way, it's like Velcro and superglue combined. He picks me up by my head and slams me into the wall. I can barely breathe anymore, and the smell of his breath is so bad at close range, I barely want to.

"Guilty as charged!" he tells me. Then he peels his grip off of me, and I drop to the floor like a load of concrete.

The Lizard King runs up the wall and across the ceiling. He hangs there, upside down, ready to deliver my sentence.

"Three rounds in the detention chamber with the Dragon Lady!" he yells. "Or until someone ends up dead, whichever comes first!"

CHAPTER 30

WHAT'S THE BIG DEAL?

Rafe, are you listening to me?"

I looked up at Mr. Dwight and nodded.

"You need to get your act together, young man. Keep up this kind of behavior and it's going to be more than just detention for you. Understood?"

I knew I couldn't talk my way out of this, so I didn't even try. "Understood," I told him, and got up to leave.

At least my trip to the principal's office was worth 30,000 points, on top of everything else I'd earned for my little "wardrobe malfunction." Pointwise, it had been a pretty good day. But Dragon Lady–wise? I felt like I was already dead.

After I left the office, guess who was the first person to come up to me in the hall? (I'll give you a hint: It's not who you think, and it rhymes with Beanie Balletta.)

"What the heck was all that?" Jeanne asked me.

"I got three detentions with Donatello," I said.

"That's not what I'm talking about," she said. "I mean, why would you want to run around school in your underwear? This whole rule-breaking thing of yours is getting kind of . . . stupid, to tell you the truth."

"You're right," I told her. "It *is* stupid. Just as stupid as some of these rules." I don't know why Jeanne was talking to me, and I don't know why I always told her everything I was thinking. Still, she didn't walk away, so I kept going. "No hats? No sunglasses? No pants that are too big or shirts that are too small? Do you really think all these rules do anything to make the school a better place?"

"That's not up to me," she said.

"But that's exactly what you said in your student council speech," I told her. "You said you wanted to make the school a better place, right?"

"I do, but—"

She stopped suddenly and looked at me like

she'd just thought of something. "That speech was two months ago. You still remember what I said?" she asked.

Oh, man. *Capital O.O.P.S.!*

Admitting something like that to a girl who would probably go out with a fire hydrant before she went out with me was even more embarrassing than the fact that she'd seen me running around in my underwear.

And I wasn't done either. The next thing to come out of my mouth went something like this:

"Yeah, well, uh . . . you know. It's not like . . . you know. I just, uh . . . well . . . uh . . . yeah. Okay . . . I probably need to, uh . . . I better . . . go now."

And then I did go—right out of there and into the Geek Hall of Fame.

One of these days, I was going to have a regular, nonembarrassing, just-be-myself, don't-do-anything-stupid conversation with Jeanne Galletta.

But today was not that day.

THIS WAY TO LOSERVILLE

CHAPTER 31

DINNER FOR THREE AT SWIFTY'S DINER

November 2 is a good day. It's Mom's birthday, and she said all she wanted this year was for us to come have dinner at Swifty's while she was working.

Still, Georgia made her a drawing (whoopee), and I used most of my Zoom money to get her a card and some of this perfume she likes. We put the gifts out on the table so they'd be sitting there when she came to take our order.

Swifty's is a pretty good place to eat. I usually get the burger with double fries, or sometimes the open-faced turkey sandwich with mashed potatoes and gravy. And we almost always get the apple pie with ice cream and extra cinnamon for dessert.

The other reason I like Swifty's is that they have Mom's paintings up on the wall for sale. She doesn't have much time to paint these days, since she's always working, but I think she's a really good artist—even if her stuff is kind of weird.

None of Mom's paintings have names. She says you're supposed to look at them and decide for yourself how they make you feel. Mostly I just feel happy when she sells one. It doesn't happen that often, but when it does, that's a good day too.

When she came up to the table, Mom smiled at the presents we'd brought her, but I could tell right away that something was wrong.

"You kids can go ahead and order," she said. "Bear called to say he couldn't make it. He's got somewhere else to be."

"On your birthday?" I asked, which I probably shouldn't have. Mom was trying to pretend like it didn't matter, but she's an artist, not an actress, if you know what I mean.

"This will be nice, just the three of us," she said. "And besides, now you can get whatever you want. Even the steak."

Usually we had to spend ten dollars or less when Bear was there, because he ate so much and Mom couldn't afford it. Talk about lame!

"Steak, please," I ordered.

"One steak, medium well with double fries," Mom said, writing it down on her pad and smiling again. "How about you, Georgia Peach?"

"Rafe was naked in school!"

It came out of her just like that. With Georgia, secrets are kind of like time bombs, and you never know when one's going to go off.

"What?" Mom said.

"Shut up!" I said. "I was not."

"Gracie said that Miranda Piccolino said her brother said you were running all over the school like that."

"I wasn't naked!" I yelled.

Just in case you're wondering, that's not a thing you want to yell in the middle of a crowded diner. I felt like every single eyeball in the place turned to look at me. Probably because they did.

Mom was looking at me too. She stood there really still, like a statue.

"It was just a Halloween thing," I said.

"Gracie said that Miranda said that her brother said you were—OUCH!"

That was me, kicking Georgia under the table. And then—

"WAHHHH!"

That was Georgia, making like a howler monkey and trying to look like she was crying, which she wasn't, the big faker.

Then the worst thing of all happened. I looked up at Mom again. She hadn't moved, but this one tear rolled down her cheek. Then she turned away and walked into the back room without saying anything at all.

"See what you did?" I told Georgia. "Way to go."

"I'm not the one who ran around NAKED!" she yelled, just in case the people in the parking lot hadn't heard it the first time.

But I didn't even care about that anymore. I was already up and following Mom.

CHAPTER 32

SCUM

Mom?"

"I'm okay," she said.

She was sitting on a big white plastic tub of dill pickle chips in the storage room. Giant containers of everything on the menu are kept back there. If you got stuck in that room, you'd never, ever starve.

"I didn't mean to make you cry," I said.

"Come over here, Rafe." She patted the empty pickle tub next to hers, just as Swifty stuck his head in the door. (Actually his name is Fred, but there was already a place called Fred's Diner on the other side of town.)

"Jules, I don't mean to be a hard guy, but we're kind of busy out here," he said.

"I'll be right there," she told him. "Promise."

Great. Now it was Bear, Swifty, and me, all giving Mom a hard time. That's not a list I wanted to be on.

"We never did finish our chat about Leonardo," Mom said. "I want you to know that I know you've been talking to him again."

"I don't have to," I told her right away. "I can stop."

"No, honey," she said. "I've been thinking about this. We all talk to people who aren't there, all the time, with texting, and computers, and even answering machines. Artists talk to their muses for inspiration. Some people even talk to themselves."

"That's true," I said. Sometimes I could hear Mom out in the garage when she was painting, talking away even though nobody else was there.

"So why shouldn't you talk to Leo if you want to?" she said. "Besides, it's not Leo I'm worried about. It's you."

"I'm okay," I insisted.

"Are you?" she asked, looking at me in that Mom way. "Sweetie, you've been getting into so much trouble at school lately. I just don't understand. I know it's been a tough year, and I haven't been around much, but . . . but . . ."

And then she started crying all over again.

On her birthday.

Because of me.

I've never felt like a bigger piece of scum than I did right then. Just one big slice of loser meat on toast. So much for being a good person.

HOW HARD COULD IT BE?

After what happened that night, I knew I had to put the game on hold. No more breaking the rules on purpose. No more Operation R.A.F.E. for the time being. No Zoom for sale, and no fighting with Bear either. If I couldn't be *good*, I could at least try to be a normal person for a while. I mean, how hard could it be?

"You're going to regret this," Leo told me. "Besides, Jules doesn't want you to be *normal*. She just wants you to be yourself. Doesn't she say that all the time?"

"Yeah, well, *myself* made his mother cry tonight," I said. "I'm just going to lie low for a while, that's all. Just until things get a little better around here."

"Sure," Leo said. "Right after you win the lottery, and Jules turns into a famous artist, and Georgia has a personality transplant, and Bear gets amnesia and never comes home. Forget it, dude. You're living in a fantasy world."

"Look who's talking," I said.

"And that's another thing," Leo told me. "What am I supposed to do while you're off being Mr. Normal?"

"I don't know," I said. "What do imaginary people do in their spare time?" Leo yawned. "I mean, it's not like I'm going anywhere. You can still talk to me. We just won't be playing the game."

"But we're only getting started here," he said. "You can't quit now."

"I'm not quitting," I told him. "I'm taking a time-out."

"For how long?"

"I don't know," I said again. "We're just going to have to wait and see, okay?"

But Leo didn't say anything.

"Okay?"

Still nothing.

"Leo?"

My whole room suddenly felt kind of . . . empty. I'd never seen Leo mad before, but I think that's what was going on now.

Leo the Silent was giving me the silent treatment.

CHAPTER 34

NORMAL

The next day at school wasn't as hard as I thought it would be. I paid extra attention to what some of the good kids were doing, and I tried to do the same stuff. (Some of it, anyway.) I showed up on time for class; I raised my hand when I thought I knew the answer, even though I was usually wrong; and I told my Zoom customers I was out of business until further notice.

In Donatello's English class, I volunteered to hand out the assignment sheets. She looked at me like nothing weirder had ever happened in her life.

"Are you trying to butter me up before your next detention?" she said. "Because it's working. Thank you, Rafe."

I just said, "You're welcome." If there was some

buttering involved, that was a bonus.

And speaking of bonuses, Jeanne Galletta actually smiled at me when I gave her the handout. I'd been avoiding her ever since the whole underwear episode on Halloween, so I was surprised when she smiled like that. Maybe it had something to do with me being normal for a change.

In fact, it seemed that the only people who didn't like me this way were Leo (no surprise) and Allison Prouty, who kept looking at me like I was ruining her career as Hills Village Middle School's number one kiss-up.

The English assignment was a vocabulary exercise. It was all about abstract nouns, or "things that aren't things," as Donatello called them. The list had words like *contentment, prosperity, fortitude, vastness,* and stuff like that. We were supposed to work in groups to find pictures that represented what the words meant to us. It made me think about how Donatello and my mom could totally hang out. They're both into all that arty stuff.

I wasn't in Jeanne's group, unfortunately, but I

was still being Normal Rafe, so I volunteered to be the recorder for my group. Matt Baumgarten and Melinda Truitt printed pictures from the computer, and Chance Freeman looked through a bunch of magazines Donatello had brought in. I cut out the stuff they found and put it all together in a big collage kind of thing. I made the pictures fit up against each other like puzzle pieces and spelled out the vocab words with letters from the magazines.

When Donatello came around to check everybody's work, she stopped and looked at ours for a long time. "This is very creative," she said. "Very organic."

All I know about organic is the disgusting plain yogurt Mom keeps in the fridge at home, but I'm pretty sure Donatello meant it was a good thing. Nobody in the group gave me credit for the idea either, and I didn't even care. I knew she was talking to me.

So this was what normal felt like. It sure wasn't as fun as Operation R.A.F.E., but if this is what it took to keep Mom happy and off my case, then I figured it would be worth it.

Too bad it lasted only one day.

CHAPTER 35

MILLER STRIKES AGAIN

If you've been reading carefully, you probably noticed a kind of pattern in my life. Just when things seem to be going okay . . . blah, blah, blah.

So there I was at my locker, feeling pretty good about how the day had gone and getting ready to go home. I had half my stuff in my backpack and the other half in my hand, when I turned around—right into a big pile of Miller. (In the future, when it's possible to have extra eyes installed in the back of your head, I'm definitely going to be the first one in line.)

He stuck out his foot, put a hand on my back, and pushed. I went down hard, along with all my stuff.

"Careful," Miller said. "You might trip and fall."

"Yeah," I said. "You're a regular baby Einstein."

"Right," he said, like he thought I was serious. "You ready for the meeting?"

"What meeting?"

"My fist, your face," he said, and pointed outside. "Come on. Once and for all, dirtbag."

I was getting tired of this. Way past tired.

Maybe dangerously past it.

"Listen, Miller," I said, "I already told you. I'm not trying to prove anything, and even if I was before, I'm done, okay? So just back off."

But he wasn't even listening anymore.

"What's this?"

He bent down and picked up something off the floor. It was my Operation R.A.F.E. notebook! I hadn't even realized it had come out of my backpack—until then.

"It's nothing," I said. "Give it back."

Miller already had it open to the first page. "Operation R.A.F.E.?" he said. "What are you? Six years old?"

"I told you, it's nothing," I said. I reached, but he pulled away.

"If it's nothing, why do you look like you're going to wet your pants?" Miller said.

I couldn't believe this was happening. This was supposed to be Normal, Day 1, and all of a sudden it was more like Worst Nightmare, Part 13.

Miller was flipping through the pages, looking at everything I'd written, and smiling like he'd just found a box of money.

And that's when I saw it happen. Miller the Killer had just gotten himself an idea. You could see it on his face. It was like watching a caveman stand up on his own two feet for the first time.

"Here you go," he said. He ripped the cover right off the notebook and handed it to me. "That much is free. The rest is a dollar."

What was I going to do—take him down with paper cuts?

"Fine," I said, and took one of the two dollars out of my pocket. "Here. Now give it to me."

But all he did was tear off the first page and hand it over.

"*What?*" he said. "You thought it was a dollar for the whole thing? What do you think I am, some kind of idiot?"

Attention! Do not answer that question! I repeat, do NOT answer that question!

"Come on, Miller," I said, not answering the question.

"Come on, Miller," he said, in this little squeaky voice, like that's how I sounded.

"I don't have the money for all that," I told him. I'd practically filled up the notebook, and there were something like seventy pages in there.

Miller just shrugged, folded it in half, and shoved it under his arm. "You can take your time," he said, walking away. "A dollar a page, Khatchadorian. Unless the price goes up, which it might."

I kind of felt like it already had. So much for normal.

CHAPTER 36

WHAT NOW?

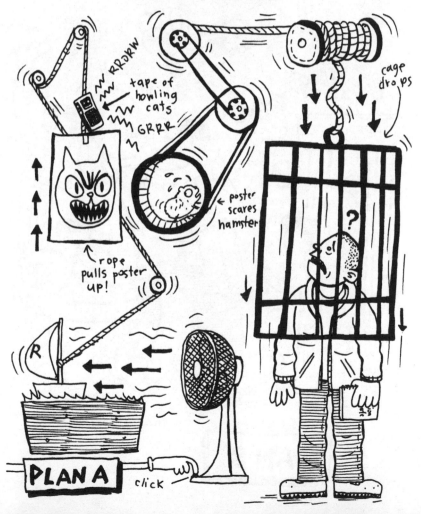

I spent the whole afternoon trying to come up with some kind of plan for how I was going to deal with Miller.

All of my ideas were great, except for the part about them being totally impossible.

And letting Miller keep the notebook just wasn't an option. I mean, if Mom acted the way she did about what happened on Halloween, what would she do if she found out about the whole Operation R.A.F.E. thing?

I had to face the facts: Miller had me, and I was going to spend the rest of sixth grade buying back that stupid notebook, one page at a time.

That meant I needed to start making some money right away. As far as I knew, there was only one way to do that, and it was sitting in brightly colored cans out in the garage.

"Yes!" Leo said as soon as I thought of it. "*That's* what I'm talking about!"

"You're back," I said.

"Never left," he said. "I was just waiting around for something interesting to happen. Oh, and by the way, you tanked your second life when Miller got that notebook away from you. Only one life left. You're going to have to be careful."

"I don't care about that right now," I said. "I just want the notebook."

"Well, then, what are you waiting for? Let's go."

"Okay," I said, and headed out toward the garage. "But I'm only selling the soda," I told Leo. "I'm not getting back in the game."

"We'll see," Leo said.

CHAPTER 37

BUSTED!

So there I was, minding my own business and stealing a few six-packs of Zoom out of the garage, when guess who came walking up on her silent little feet to spy on me?

"What are you doing?" Georgia asked. "You're not supposed to be out here. Are you taking that? Why are you taking that?"

"Close the door!" I told her. I knew that would be faster than trying to get her to go away.

"Bear's going to kill you," she said.

"Not if he doesn't find out." I put another six-pack in my backpack and then stepped up really close, so I was looking straight down at her. "Understood?"

She tried to look past me. "Why do you need so much?" she said.

"Why are you on his side?" I asked.

"I'm not!" she said right away. I knew that would get her. She hates Bear as much as I do.

"Listen," I told her. "Every time I take some of this, I'll take one for you too. We can drink it when Bear's asleep and Mom's not around."

She looked first at me, and then at the cases of Zoom under the workbench, and then back at me. "You've done this before, haven't you?" she said.

"Do you want it or not?" I said, holding up the can. The thing is, Georgia likes soda even more than secrets, and Mom hardly ever lets us drink it.

"What if we get caught?" she said.

"We won't," I told her. "Not if we keep our mouths shut and don't say anything."

"Okay."

"*Ever*," I said.

"*O-kaaay*," she promised, looking at the can instead of me. I took her by the shoulders and made her sit down on an old milk crate.

"For Mom's sake," I said. "Swear?"

"I swear, I swear," she insisted. "Triple swear."

That was only a double, but I let her go.

Even with all that promising, there was no

guarantee. Not with Georgia, but it was too late now. She'd already busted me, and this was my best shot at keeping her quiet.

I was just going to have to take my chances.

CHAPTER 38

THE DARK AGES

If you ask me, one of the worst parts of the school year is between Halloween and Thanksgiving. You've been there long enough to know how bad it can be, but Christmas break isn't nearly soon enough, and the end of the year is nowhere in sight.

It's also right after daylight saving time, so when you leave in the morning, it's dark, and when you get home after school, it's practically dark.

Dark, dark, dark . . . that was my life these days.

When I showed up for the first of those three Wednesday detentions with Donatello, I found out she'd done the same thing as before. It was going to be just me and the Dragon Lady, all alone, for the whole hour.

That could mean only one thing: I was dragon chow.

I don't want to eat you. Just talk to me.

I also started selling Zoom out of my locker again, but it wasn't the same anymore. The stakes were higher. I couldn't afford to get caught, so I couldn't do it all the time. Plus, Bear's stash was starting to get too low. I ended up spending more than half of what I made just putting new cans back in the garage so he wouldn't notice.

Back in detention again, I did my best to keep Donatello from slicing and dicing my brain into little pieces, but it wasn't easy. She kept trying to get me to talk about myself, and I kept telling her I had homework to do. Sometimes that worked. Sometimes it didn't.

Then there was Miller. You'd think he'd give me some credit for the whole break-every-rule-in-the-book thing, but no. He just thought I was trying to prove I was a bigger criminal than he was. Talk about paranoid. I had to tell him ahead of time how many pages I wanted to buy, and then he'd just show up with that many.

I didn't get very far either. With the way I had to keep restocking Bear's stash, I only managed to buy eighteen pages before Thanksgiving.

On top of everything else, I was still trying to be Normal Rafe and not get into any more trouble. It was working, I guess, but I still wasn't any good at school and still hated my classes as much as ever. I thought being normal would make me feel like a better person, but so far? Not really.

But here's the funny part. Even though I felt like I was still living in the Dark Ages, nobody seemed to notice. As far as Mom, and Jeanne, and even Donatello were concerned, I'd already turned over a whole new leaf.

And if you're wondering about Leo, let's just say
he thought I was getting exactly what I deserved.

CHAPTER 39

JEANNE, JEANNE, JEANNE

Don't think I haven't noticed," Jeanne said to me on the Monday before Thanksgiving.

I turned around with water dripping off my face from the fountain. "Noticed what?" I said, wiping it away. On the outside, I was just standing there, but on the inside I was thinking: HOLYCOWIT'S JEANNEYOUCANDOTHISRAFEJUSTSTAY COOLANDDON'TDOANYTHINGSTUPID!

"You've been playing by the rules," Jeanne said, but she whispered it like we had this secret between us, which we kind of did. She was one of the only people who knew about Operation R.A.F.E.

"I'm on a break," I told her. "I'm just being normal for a while."

"Yeah," she said. "That's what I noticed. So let me ask you something: What are you doing after school on Wednesday?"

"Nothing," I said in about a split second.

"That was quick," she said. "Are you sure?"

"Yep."

It didn't seem possible, but I couldn't help wondering if the impossible was about to happen. Was Jeanne Galletta really about to ask me to go out with her?

"Well, good," she said. "Because student council is doing a fund-raiser at the Duper Market. We're sponsoring a family who can't afford their own Thanksgiving. There's going to be a pie-and-cookie sale, and a food drive too. We could really use some extra help."

"Oh," I said. "Well, um . . . yeah . . . okay. Sounds like a good cause." (What else was I going to say?)

"Great!" Jeanne said. "Three thirty on Wednesday. And if you could ask your mom or dad to make something for the bake sale, that would be awesome."

"Sure," I told her. "My mom makes these really good apple pies all the time, with lots of cinnamon. I'll bring one of those."

"Thanks, Rafe, I really appreciate it," Jeanne said. Then before she left, she leaned in again, really close, and whispered, "I like you like this. And don't worry. Your secret's safe with me."

Before I could say anything, or do something to mess it up, she was already walking away. And I thought—

Hmmmm . . .

CHAPTER 40

CHARITY CASE

This was a real first. Nobody in the history of Rafe Khatchadorian had ever asked me to help out at a charity thing before. When I told Mom about it, she thought it was great and got Swifty to donate a pie from the diner, no problem. I showed up at the Duper Market with it on Wednesday afternoon.

"Rafe! You're here!" Jeanne said. She was like the queen bee in the middle of it all. There was a big table set up outside with bake sale stuff, and a huge bin where people coming out of the market could drop food donations. She also had a jar in the middle of the table that said THANK YOU on it.

"Here's something else," I said, and dropped ten dollars that I couldn't afford in the jar, from that week's Zoom sales.

"Wow!" Jeanne's eyes opened wide, like she was really impressed, and my heart went a little faster. (Okay, a lot faster.) "So, we're trying to let people around the neighborhood know about the sale. We've got these big signs, and we're handing out flyers everywhere. Do you think you could—?"

"I'm on it," I told her.

"Great!" she said. Then she reached under the table and took out what looked like about fifteen pounds of orange fur. "We got this from the high school. It's kind of big, but I think it'll fit you," she said.

It was the costume for the Hills Village High School mascot—an orange falcon with wings, a big yellow beak, and a blue superhero cape.

"This will really get people's attention," Jeanne said.

"You're kidding, right?" One look at her face told me she wasn't. "I mean, uh . . . sure," I said. "Anything for charity."

"Thanks, Rafe, you're the best."

I tried to smile.

It's a good thing that costume covered my face, because I was about sixteen shades of red once

I put the whole thing on. As I walked across the Duper Market parking lot, I'm pretty sure the laughing I heard was a whole lot more *at* me than *with* me. Especially considering that I wasn't laughing—not even a little.

But I'll tell you something else. Once I got out there on the sidewalk and realized that nobody knew who the heck I was (just like with the ninja), I started getting kind of into it.

I flapped my wings, and jumped around with my sign, and gave out flyers, and patted people on the back when they took them. Drivers honked their horns as they went by, and some of them even pulled in when I pointed the way. If I do say so myself, I was just about the world's most awesome bake-sale mascot ever.

And don't think Jeanne didn't notice, because she did.

"You were amazing," she said afterward. "Thanks again, Rafe."

I liked that she thought I was amazing. It kind of made me *feel* amazing. Not only was Jeanne Galletta smiling at me like crazy, but I'd just spent the afternoon doing the kind of stuff that good people (not just normal people, but *good* people) do.

Maybe that's where I got my nerve to say what I said next.

"Do you want to go get some pizza after this?" I asked her. "My mom could drive you home later, and I'm starving."

"Oh," Jeanne said. In fact, that's all she said at first. And she wasn't smiling anymore. "Listen, Rafe—"

"I think you're really nice. Some of the time, anyway," she said. "But I don't want you to get the wrong idea. It just seemed like you were . . . I don't know . . . changing, and I thought it might be good for you to—"

"To what?" I said. I was really embarrassed, but I was also a little bit mad, and getting madder.

"You know," she said. "To join in with school stuff, that kind of thing."

"You thought it would be . . . *good for me*?" I said. "Like I'm your little project, or something?"

"I didn't mean it that way," she said.

Then Allison Prouty called over from her mom's minivan. "Hey, Jay-Gee, are you coming?" That's what the popular kids called her, Jay-Gee for *Jeanne Galletta*. There were a bunch of them in the backseat.

"I have to go, Rafe," she told me. "Please don't take what I said personally. I *really* appreciate what you did today."

"Sure," I said. "Did you get extra credit for it too?"

"Jeanne!" Allison yelled. "Come on!"

"I really do have to go," she said. "Have a good

Thanksgiving, Rafe. I'll see you next week."

"Whatever," I said, but she was already gone.

I may have been dressed as a falcon, but I'll tell you what. I felt like the biggest Thanksgiving turkey in the world.

CHAPTER 41

REPORT CARD TIME—
ALL A'S—YAY!

Not a lot changed between Thanksgiving and Christmas break. In fact, if I tried to tell you too much about it, you'd just think the pages of this book had stuck together and you were reading the same chapters all over again. So here's the short version:

Miller was a bottom-feeding, scum-of-the-earth dipwad—always. I had to keep some of my Zoom money to buy Christmas presents, so I only managed to get another twelve pages out of him.

And as for school? The last thing Ms. Donatello said to me before vacation was, "Keep trying, Rafe. I know you can do better. And I know you know it too." In other words, don't expect any good news on your report card.

That's why I spent the first couple of afternoons of winter break outside in the cold, waiting for the mailman to come. Mom was always at work in the afternoon, and Bear never noticed anything unless it was on TV or had pepperoni on it, so I was all covered there.

On the third day, we got an envelope with an HVMS return address in the corner and the smell of doom all over it. I stuck it inside my coat, dropped the rest of the mail inside, and went straight to my room to check out the damage.

REPORT CARD HVMS Name: **RAFE K.**

SUBJECT	GRADE	NOTES/COMMENTS
Social Studies	F	Who needs social studies anyway?
English	D	D is for Donatello!
Science	D-	Science is for geeks.
Math	F	Thanks for playing. Better luck next time!
Spanish	F	I'm barely passing English!
Gym	D+	Dude? A D+ in gym?! How hard can it be?
Art	C	Way to go! GENIUS!

There was also a letter for Mom, signed by Mrs. Stricker. It said she was going to "be in touch" after vacation so they could "schedule a conference" to talk about "Rafe's academic performance."

Oh, man. It was worse than I thought.

Basically, I had two options. I could get this over with fast and leave my report card on the counter where Mom would see it. Or . . . I could buy some time. That way, at least Mom would have a half-decent Christmas without having to worry about me for a while. She deserved it and, to tell you the truth, I felt like I did too.

My first idea was to just shove everything way under my mattress, but Leo never likes it when I do anything halfway.

"Why take chances?" he said. "There are a lot of better ways to make things disappear than that."

He was right, of course, so I changed plans. I stuck it all back inside my coat, made a quick stop in the kitchen, and then picked up Ditka's leash from the hook by the back door.

"Ditka! Here, boy!"

There are exactly two ways to make friends with Ditka—food and walks. As soon as he saw that leash in my hand, he came running like a four-legged linebacker and pinned me to the door, slobbering all over the place.

"Where you going, Squirt?" Bear asked from the couch.

"Just taking Ditka for a walk," I said, like it was something I did all the time.

"Sounds good," he said. "You could both use the exercise."

Look who's talking, I thought.

"See you later," I said, and we took off.

Walking Ditka isn't really like walking at all. It's more like getting dragged behind a tank and trying to steer. Luckily, Ditka works on autopilot and went right over to this field where he likes to do his business. A bunch of condos were supposed to be built there, but the lot was mostly deserted in the meantime.

At the back of the field, there's a drainage ditch with a stream running into a big pipe at the bottom. I tied Ditka's leash to a tree when we got there, and I went down by the water, where nobody could see me.

Next, I found some rocks and made a circle

next to the water, like a little campfire. Then I took out my report card, the letter from Mrs. Stricker, the envelope, and a box of wooden kitchen matches from home. I'm not usually supposed to do anything with fire when Mom's not around but, then again, I'm not usually supposed to incinerate my report card either. I crumpled it all up in the middle of the circle and lit it.

Once it was done, just ashes, I kicked everything into the water and watched it wash down the drainpipe. Then I scuffed up the ground so there wouldn't be any footprints, untied Ditka, and let him drag me home the long way around the block, just in case anyone was watching. It was all kinds of overkill, but like Leo said, why take chances?

And guess what? It worked. (For a little while, anyway.)

CHAPTER 43

SHORT AND SWEET, BUT MOSTLY JUST SHORT

Okay, that's not exactly what Christmas looked like but, to tell you the truth, it could have been a lot worse. No major disasters, anyway.

The weirdest part was having Bear around on Christmas morning for the first time. Mom knew Georgia and I wouldn't want to buy presents for him, so she got some little stuff and put our names on the tags. For her sake, I didn't say anything about it. I just said "you're welcome" when he opened the NFL foam can holders I supposedly got for him, and "thank you" when I opened the Chicago Bears sweatshirt he supposedly got for me.

After that, Mom made a really good Christmas dinner, including two kinds of pie from the diner—

apple and chocolate cream. I had firsts, seconds, and thirds of everything, and we all stayed up late watching *Raiders of the Lost Ark* on TV.

Then Christmas was over.

And then Mom found out about my grades, and the hard stuff started all over again.

(Notice how fast this chapter went by? That's exactly how it felt to me. Mom calls that "art imitating life," but I just call it my own rotten luck.)

CHAPTER 44

LOST AND FOUND

Mom was sitting at the computer when I came out to the kitchen that morning. As soon as I saw what she was doing, I knew I was toast. She was looking at the Hills Village Middle School website.

And there were my grades, right on the screen.

"Weren't we supposed to get these in the mail?" Mom said.

"Uh . . . I think so," I said, trying not to panic, or sound like someone who had burned his own report card in a ditch somewhere.

Bear was leaning against the counter with half a piece of leftover pie in one hand, a gallon of milk in the other, and Ditka licking crumbs off the floor around his feet. "Nice grades, Squirt," he said.

"These aren't too good, honey," Mom said. "What happened?"

It was another one of those questions without any good answers. I said the first thing I thought of.

"Maybe they're teaching the wrong subjects?"

It was probably true, but it wasn't going to get me out of this. Mom just looked at the screen again and sighed, like she was watching a sad movie.

"Well, in any case," she said, "we can't let these slide."

"In other words," Bear butted in, "your mother's been way too easy on you for too long. Those days are over."

"That's not what I meant," Mom said, but Bear kept yapping.

"So here's what's going to happen. Once you're back in school, you're going to come straight home every day. Then you're going to do your homework before anything else, and I'm going to check it to make sure that you do."

"*What?*" I said.

"'Fraid so, little man."

"Forget it," I said. "You're not my teacher, and you're not my father, okay?"

This was way over the line, even for Bear. I looked at Mom to back me up, but I could tell right away she wasn't going to.

"I have to work in the afternoons, Rafe. I can't be here to do everything."

"You could if he had a job," I said.

"Yo, I'm standing right here," Bear said. "And believe it or not, I was in middle school once too."

"Yeah, in the zoo."

"Watch your mouth, Squirt."

"That's another thing," I said. "Don't call me Squirt."

"Don't tell me what to do," Bear growled. "Squirt."

I felt like I wanted to explode, but Mom got there first. She threw her hands up in the air and yelled something that sounded like "AUUGH!" Then she said, "Can't you two ever have a normal conversation, just once?"

"Talk to him," Bear said. "The kid's impossible." He took the last piece of pie

out of the tray and shoved the whole thing into his mouth.

Mom got up and threw open the fridge. "You know what? You two are just going to have to work this out," she said. "Actually, scratch that. I don't care if you work it out or not. Rafe, this is the new arrangement. Carl *will* be checking your homework, and that's that."

I expected her to say something else, like "And as for *you*, Carl . . . ," but she didn't. She just got out some eggs and started making breakfast, like nothing had happened.

Like she hadn't just turned me into bear food.

And I thought, *I gave up my mission for you.*

Mom had always been the one real person I felt like I could trust. Even after Bear moved in with us, I figured she'd still be on my side when it really counted. Now I didn't know what to think anymore, except—*GET ME OUT OF HERE!*

FIRST-DAY-BACK BLUES

The first day back at school started with a bang. Or, I guess, with a shove. Miller literally nabbed me two seconds after I walked in the door. There were tons of people around, and I didn't even know he was there until I felt that familiar hand clamping onto the back of my neck.

"Guess what, Khatchadorian? I actually read some of your stupid little notebook on vacation," he said, right in my ear. "All I can say is—wow. You're even more pathetic than I thought."

"Get off of me!" I tried to pull away, but he just held on tighter. I could practically feel his greasy thumb poking into my brain stem.

"So here's the deal," Miller said. "New year, new price. It's a dollar fifty a page from now on. And if you're lucky, I won't show your girlfriend Jeanne Galletta how you like to draw little pictures of her all the time. Got it?"

He didn't wait for an answer, though. He just pushed me straight down, hard enough for a full face-plant in front of everyone.

"Watch your step, Picasso," he said.

Gabe Wisznicki gave him a high five for that one, and they both walked right over my stuff and up the hall.

Ever since Miller had gotten my notebook and started taking my money, he wasn't so interested in actually killing me anymore. It was more like he was just testing me now, to see how much I'd take.

And I guess the answer was—*this* much.

CALM   ANNOYED   MAD   ENRAGED   NOW   BOOM

I didn't stop to think. I didn't "use my words." I just got up and ran straight at Miller. My feet left the floor. I landed on his back, and I held on with everything I had.

Miller tried to reach for me, but then he changed his mind. He turned halfway around instead and jumped backward, really hard, into the wall. If it was a wrestling move, you'd call it the Dead Meat Sandwich—and guess who was the meat? I lost my grip, along with all the air in my lungs, and hit the floor (again) without Miller ever putting a hand on me.

A bunch of people gathered around. Some of them started yelling, "Fight, fight, fight," and Mrs. Stricker was out of the front office like somebody had shot her out of a cannon.

"What's going on here?" she yelled.

"Rafe jumped Miller!" Gabe said. The problem was, it was true. There were about three dozen witnesses.

"Miller pushed me down!" I said.

"You tripped," Miller said, and pointed at the mats by the front door. They're all old and warpy, and people trip on them all the time.

"Liar!"

"Wimp!"

"Both of you," Stricker said, laser tagging us with her eyes. "Into the office. Pronto!"

"But I didn't do anything!" Miller said, all wide-eyed and innocent. Seriously, they should recruit him for Drama Club.

At least Stricker wasn't buying it. "Mr. Miller, you're one of the two biggest troublemakers I've got," she told him, and then looked right at me so we'd all know who the other one was. "Let's go. March!"

I didn't have much choice, so I marched—right out of Miller the Killer's hands and into Sergeant Stricker's.

CHAPTER 46

DOING TIME WITH SERGEANT STRICKER

The cuffs dig into my wrists. My hands are numb. Sweat trickles down my forehead, and some blood too, where the guards roughed me up before they threw me into this hole.

How long have I been here? An hour? Six hours? A day? It's all a blur.

Suddenly, a bright light shines in my face. It's so strong I can't see anything else. The heat is intense.

A door opens somewhere. I can't see anyone, but I hear footsteps and jangling keys. Then a voice.

"You got something to prove, Prisoner 2041588?"

I'd know that voice anywhere. It belongs to Sergeant Ida P. Stricker, the biggest, baddest, meanest guard in this whole joint. And the *P* stands for *Pain*.

"No, ma'am," I say. "Nothing to prove."

If you forget to say "ma'am," she takes out one of your fingernails or toenails, the hard way—with a pair of pliers. Believe me, it's not a mistake you make more than once.

"Word on the cell block is that you jumped Miller the Killer for no reason," she says.

"That's 'cause you got only half the story," I say. "They left out the part about Miller starting it. *Ma'am*."

"So you're a liar *and* a fighter, is that it?"

"No, ma'am. Miller's just out to get me, that's all."

As far as I know, they've already let Miller go. This place isn't exactly the world capital of justice.

Sergeant Stricker leans in close. I can see her face now, and the long, jagged scar down her cheek.

They say she used to do cage fighting before she worked here.

"Listen up, kid. I'm on your side," she says, like I'm supposed to believe that. "I just want you to live up to your potential, that's all."

"My potential, ma'am?" I say.

"That's right. Your potential to be the youngest little hoodlum I ever sent up to the federal penitentiary." She laughs in my face, but there's no smile to go with it. "You think this place is hard, 2041588? You ain't seen nothing yet."

I think that's supposed to scare me, but it doesn't. What scares me are the brass knuckles she's unclipping from her utility belt. The ones she's sliding over her tattooed fingers right now.

"We're done talking," she says. "Time for you to go to sleep. Say night-night, 2041588."

Then she slugs me once . . . twice . . . three times before the room starts to spin, and everything goes black.

CHAPTER 47

DOWN THE DRAIN

nce Mrs. Stricker finished lecturing me about bad choices and wrong paths and good manners (huh?), she left me there in the Box. That's what we call the homework room at school. It's this tiny little room with no windows except in the door so they can keep an eye on you when you're taking a makeup test or if you're in big trouble, like I was.

After a while, one of the secretaries came in and told me they were ready for me in Mrs. Stricker's office. "*They?*" I said, but she just motioned at the door like I should stop taking up so much of her day and start moving.

By the time I got to the office, I'd figured it out for myself. Not that it mattered anymore.

It was too late to do anything about it now.
The Stealth Mom had already hit.
"Sit down, Rafe," Mom said. "We have to talk."

BLAM!

The next forty-five minutes in
that office was about as much fun
as a day at Disney World—
when it's pouring rain.

LAUNCH
STEALTH
MOM!

And all there is to eat
are hot-dog buns.
And you get electrocuted
on the rides.

Mom and Mrs. Stricker asked me a whole bunch of *thinking* questions, like "What were you *thinking*?" and "What do you *think* we should do now?"

Then they sent me back out so they could talk some more. Then they brought me in again. I was starting to feel like a human yo-yo.

"Rafe, it's time for some specific next steps," Mrs. Stricker said. "We take fighting very seriously here at Hills Village. Tomorrow, you'll have a one-day in-school suspension and, frankly, it's the least you deserve."

IMPACT IN 3...2...

"As for your grades," Mom said, "Mrs. Stricker thinks, and I agree, that some tutoring could be good for you. Ms. Donatello has already offered to work with you after school on Tuesdays and Thursdays, and I told her you'll be there."

"You'll also have a peer tutor," Mrs. Stricker

said. "Somebody your own age, to help you out with math and science once a week. We have an excellent program here at school, and I know just the student for the job."

She looked at her watch and then leaned over her phone and pushed a button. "Mrs. Harper, could you please ask Jeanne Galletta to come down to the office?"

CHAPTER 48

YOU TELL ME

Mom and Bear got into a big fight that
afternoon when she told him what had
happened. He kept yelling about how she wasn't
"hard enough" on me, and she kept telling him to
back off. I just stayed in my room, wishing for it to
be over. Finally, Mom said something about how
she was late for work, and she slammed the door
on her way out.

At least it was quiet now. At least that. I guess.

When I asked Leo what he thought I should do
about all this, he answered right away. "What is
there to think about?" he said. "Dude, you are all
out of reasons for staying out of the game, and we
both know it."

It was true. I'd spent the last two months trying

to be someone else—someone normal, maybe even someone good—and I wasn't any better off than before. Mom was mad at me, Bear was more in my face than ever, and the two of them were arguing about me all the time. Not only that, but Miller was still alive, Jeanne was about to be my tutor, and I was officially one of the worst kids in school. At least when I was playing Operation R.A.F.E., I had some fun while I was being miserable.

Hmmm . . . miserable and fun? Or miserable and no fun? You tell me.

I opened my backpack and dug in the bottom for my HVMS rule book. I hadn't even looked at it in weeks. "Where do I start?" I said.

"Anywhere," Leo said. "Just pick something and go."

"Easy for you to say," I told him. "All you have to do is come up with the ideas and then sit back. I'm the one who has to do all the work."

"How about this?" he said. "I'll give you twenty-five thousand points for your fight with Miller."

"That wasn't much of a real fight," I said. If it had been, I probably would have left school on a whole bunch of stretchers—one for each piece of me.

"You got into trouble for fighting, so you get the points for fighting," Leo said. "Plus another seventy-five thousand for the suspension. Not bad, right? Now all you have to do is earn another twenty thousand by the end of the day tomorrow, and you can consider yourself fully reactivated."

"You mean the day after tomorrow," I said. "I'm locked up in the Box all day tomorrow."

"Exactly," Leo said. "That's your welcome-back challenge."

I should have figured. It's always something with Leo.

"How am I supposed to make twenty thousand points sitting alone in a room?" I said, but Leo just sat back and pointed at the rule book in my hand.

"You tell me."

CHAPTER 49

COPYCAT

A little while later I came out to the living room, where Bear was eating Fruity Pebbles out of the box and watching some highlights from all the New Year's bowl games he'd already seen.

"I have to go to the store," I said.

"There're some fish sticks in the freezer," he said.

"It's not for dinner," I told him. "I have to go to Office Mart. I need some poster board for a school project."

"What kind of project?" he said, like I was lying (which I was, but he had no way of knowing that).

I looked over at the TV, and the scores for all the different games were flashing by. "Statistics," I said. "It's a math project."

I'd bet anything that if Bear hadn't just made himself the almighty ruler of my homework, he would have rolled over, farted, and told me this was my problem. But instead he got up and yelled for Georgia to put on her coat because we had to go to the store.

"There're fish sticks in the freezer!" she yelled back.

Fifteen minutes later, we all pulled into the parking lot outside Office Mart. I told them I'd go get my poster board and be right back.

"I want to come!" Georgia said.

"Just wait here," I told her. "Bear's missing his game highlights, and the faster I go, the faster we can get home again."

"Just park it, Georgia," Bear said.

Seriously, I was getting pretty good at this stuff.

I ran in and went straight over to the self-service copiers. Before anyone could tell me not to, I lifted up the lid on one of the machines, put my face down on the glass, and pushed the button.

The first copy came out with my nose all mashed flat, but I got it right on the second try, which was a good thing, because the manager told me to stop copying my face (even though I was paying for it).

It was eighty cents for the two color copies, plus another $2.29 for the poster board that I didn't really need. That meant two more pages I couldn't buy off of Miller, but I'd make it back once I started selling Zoom again.

"Took you long enough," Bear said when I came back to the car. I kept the photocopies pressed flat against the back of the poster board, where he couldn't see them, and got in.

"All set for tomorrow?" he said.

"Guess I'll find out tomorrow," I said, which was absolutely true.

CHAPTER 50

IT WAS WORTH A SHOT, ANYWAY

It's a documented fact that in-school suspension is the most insanely boring thing that can happen to a person at Hills Village Middle School. It's just you, your homework, and the homework room.

All. Day. Long.

I turned thirteen in that room. Winter ended, and then spring came and went. Wars happened. Trees grew. Babies were born and people died.

I now completely understand why the school gives suspensions, because by the time you get out of there, you NEVER WANT TO SPEND ANOTHER WHOLE DAY IN THAT LITTLE ROOM AGAIN. I knew I didn't.

But I did earn my 20,000 points.

Okay, truthfully? I didn't expect for one second that my whole mask idea was actually going to work—and it didn't. But it was all I could come up with on short notice, and then once I'd thought of it, I started getting all curious and wanted to give it a try anyway. Mom says every masterpiece comes at the end of a long line of failures. Maybe someday I'll get this one right and sell a zillion of them.

Meanwhile, I barely got to close my eyes before

I heard the homework room door open and Mrs. Stricker start yelling at me.

"Rafe Khatchadorian, what in heaven's name is that supposed to be? Take it off immediately!"

I did, but when I handed it over to her, something totally unexpected happened. She looked down at the mask (it was just a piece of paper with a string, really), and her face started getting all weird. Her eyes squinched up. Her cheeks got kind of twitchy. At first I thought something was wrong, but then she just burst out laughing.

It didn't last long, maybe two or three seconds before she got control of herself. Then she cleared her throat once, told me to get back to work, and left the room shaking her head.

Now, I don't know if you can appreciate this without actually knowing her, but getting Mrs. Stricker to laugh is like getting an octopus to stand up on two legs. And maybe juggle with the other six. As far as I know, nobody's ever seen it happen in the history of HVMS.

That's why Leo gave me the 20,000 points anyway.

And *that's* the story of how I survived my first in-school suspension.

CHAPTER 51

TWO TO TUTOR

That next Wednesday at lunch was supposed
to be my first tutoring session with Jeanne.
I spent all of Mr. Rourke's fourth-period social
studies trying to make myself throw up or pass out
just by thinking about it, but all I got was dizzy.

After the bell I went to my locker, even though
I already had my math book. Then I went to the
bathroom, even though I didn't have to go. Then I
went and got lunch, even though I wasn't hungry.
And *then* I slowly walked toward the math room.

I'd already asked Mrs. Stricker for a different
tutor, but basically, unless Jeanne was a convicted
serial killer, or at least had head lice, I was stuck
with her.

When I got to the math room door, my feet just

kind of kept going straight up the hall, like they knew better. Maybe I'd circle back around and try again, I thought. Or maybe . . . not even that.

"Rafe?" I looked back, and Jeanne was leaning out into the hall. "Are you about to blow me off?" she said.

She sure does cut to the chase, I'll tell you that much.

"No, I just wanted to get something out of my locker," I said.

"Uh-huh," she said, but it sounded a lot like *Suuuuure you did*. "Listen, Rafe, it's just tutoring. I can take it if you can."

I can take it if you can? How was I supposed to back out now?

"Sure," I told her. "No problem."

I followed her inside, and we sat down at one of the worktables. Jeanne already had her math book out. "You're on unit eight, right?" she said.

"I guess so," I said.

"Dividing fractions. That's a hard one."

I knew she was just trying to be nice. She'd probably finished unit eight when she *was* eight, and here I was, still trying to get through it.

Fractions are yummy! Open up!

MATH

She took out
a pencil and started pointing
at a bunch of fractions on the page. "So, you see
these top numbers?" she said. "That's called the
numerator. And then these bottom ones are—"

I didn't even know I was about to say something.

"I'll give you five dollars if we can skip this and
pretend like we didn't," I told her. It just kind of
popped out.

Jeanne raised one eyebrow. I wasn't sure what
that meant. She kept looking at me for a long time,

until I started to wonder if it was a staring contest or something.

Then she said, "Just so you know, Rafe, I never thought you were my 'project,' or whatever. I was just trying to be nice."

Whoa. I was surprised she even remembered I'd said that. The whole Thanksgiving bake sale disaster seemed like ancient history by now, and we'd never talked about it at all, which was kind of awkward.

But you know what was even more awkward? Talking about it.

Besides, I was done with letting Jeanne see me as a loser. In fact, I was starting to feel done with a lot of things these days.

"I didn't think you really thought that," I said, even though I really did. "It's no big deal." Jeanne just kept looking at me, so I opened my backpack and took out my math book, some paper, and a pencil. "Go ahead," I said. "What do you call those top numbers again?"

She picked up her pencil too. "Are you sure you want to do this?" she said.

"Sure," I said. "I can take it if you can."

CHAPTER 52

PLAY-BY-PLAY

WELCOME BACK, OPERATION R.A.F.E. fans!

This game is coming to you **LIVE** from **HVMS**, where we're in the 3rd quarter of action and the score is

RAFE KHATCHADORIAN: 910,000, and

... **H**ills Village: 0! Khatchadorian's been showing some fine form this quarter. A lot of people might have thought he was out for good after that stumble in the first half, but he's come back strong. We've been watching some world-class play ever since. Let's go to the highlights."

"Remember, folks, it's not just getting it done in this game. It's how you do it. Rafe's coach, Leo the Silent, has insisted on nothing but technique, technique, technique, and Khatchadorian has risen to the occasion. He's not just back, ladies and gentlemen. He's better than ever!"

"Of course, the question on everyone's mind is whether Khatchadorian can break every last rule in the book and advance to the final round before the year is over. According to our latest R.A.F.E.-Net poll, seventy-two percent of you out there think he's going to pull this one out in the end. I'll tell you this much, ladies and gentlemen—judging by the quality of his third-quarter play, it looks like he just might do it!"

"We've been hearing a lot of talk from Khatchadorian about some kind of huge finish coming up at the end of this game. Whether that's just the usual trash talk or whether there's some real action to back it up, we'll have to wait and find out. One thing's for sure, though: Rafe's biggest obstacles are still ahead of him. Will he crash and burn? Or will he go out in a blaze of glory? All we can tell you right now, ladies and gentlemen, is that we're going to keep with this story until it's over, one way or another. So stay tuned!"

CHAPTER 53

TUESDAYS AND THURSDAYS

I'm not sure what the difference was supposed to be between *tutoring* with Donatello and *detention* with Donatello, but it felt a whole lot to me like I'd gotten a bunch of detentions just for being dumb.

Most of the time, we did regular class work, like diagramming sentences (yawn) or research for my social studies report on copper mining (yawn . . . *zzzzzz*). But one Tuesday after school, I came in and she had a bunch of big sketch pads and pencils and markers out on the table.

"What's all this?" I asked.

"I thought you could use a little break," she said. "We're just going to sketch today." Then she picked up a pad for herself, and I realized she really meant *we*.

"You look surprised," she said. "I love sketching.

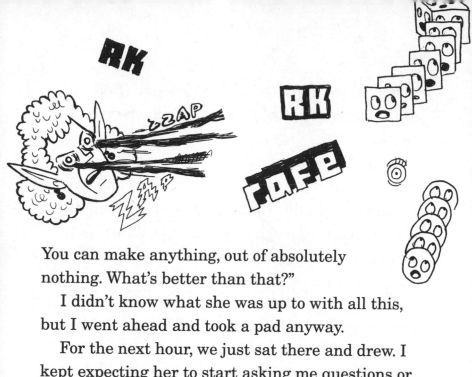

You can make anything, out of absolutely nothing. What's better than that?"

I didn't know what she was up to with all this, but I went ahead and took a pad anyway.

For the next hour, we just sat there and drew. I kept expecting her to start asking me questions or to give me some kind of assignment, but she never did. When the bell rang for late bus, she just asked to see what I'd done. It was definitely the best not-quite-a-detention I'd ever had.

"You've got a wonderful imagination," Donatello said, looking at my stuff. "It's all right there on the page."

For a second, it made me want to tell her about Leo. Most of what was "on the page" felt like it came from him. But Donatello probably thought I was messed up enough as it was. She didn't need to hear about me getting ideas from someone who wasn't even there.

When she was done looking, I started to tear out my pages, but she told me to keep the whole pad.

"Put it to good use, okay?" she said. "Nice job today, Rafe. Excellent, in fact."

I wasn't sure whether I should take the pad or not. It felt like some kind of test, and I didn't know what the right answer was.

"But we didn't do anything today," I said.

Donatello just shrugged. "I guess that depends on how you look at it."

I had to go. The late-bus driver was always super-strict about leaving on time, and I didn't want to walk home. So I went ahead and took the sketch pad. I still wasn't sure if that's what I was supposed to do or not, but Donatello wasn't telling.

CHAPTER 54

SPECIAL ASSIGNMENT

I was getting close.

Close to the end of the rule book, close to getting all my pages back from Miller, and at least kind of close to the end of the year. The weather was warming up, and pretty soon it was going to be time to start thinking about that final project.

But first there was one other thing I wanted to do.

This wasn't for points. Or for Leo. It was just for me, and it was going to take all my skills to pull it off, everything I'd used in the game so far—art, stealth, and bravery. The Big Three.

I'd already put together my materials (six bucks for a hundred black-and-white copies at Office Mart) and brought them to school that morning. Now here I was, sitting through first-period Spanish, ready to make my next move.

In Señor Wasserman's class, you can almost always get a bathroom pass, as long as you ask for it in Spanish. So I'd practiced the night before.

"Señor Wasserman, me permite ir al baño?" I said.

"Sí, Rafael," he told me.

The tricky part wasn't getting the pass. It was getting those copies I'd brought to school out of

the room without anyone seeing. And that's why
I already had a stack of them shoved down the
back of my boxers. It didn't matter if the paper got
wrinkled. In fact, I kind of like how it worked out,
seeing as how this whole plan was all about getting
back at the biggest butt-face in the entire school.

CHAPTER 55

IS IT STILL BULLYING IF YOU'RE BULLYING THE BULLY?

By lunchtime, I'd gotten four different hall passes and hit up most of the boys' bathrooms, two of the girls' bathrooms, the back of the library, and a bunch of the second-floor lockers, all without being caught. Not only had everyone seen my flyers by now, but they were all talking about them too.

It wasn't like I expected people to actually buy this idea, that Miller was any kind of chicken, killer or otherwise. Still, I had a feeling the nickname was going to stick for a while.

That took care of the offense part of my plan. Now it was time to switch to defense.

I hadn't laid eyes on Miller since homeroom, but

it didn't take a genius to know I'd be at the top of his suspect list. In fact, he was probably looking for me right then. So I went looking for him.

He and his friends almost always hung out in the hall outside the gym at lunch and, sure enough, there they were. My heart was pounding big-time as I walked up to them.

Ricky Peña saw me first and elbowed Miller. When Miller turned around, I could see one of my flyers crumpled up in his hand—not to mention the murder in his eyes.

He came right for me.

"I didn't do it!" I said. He grabbed me by the shirt anyway, but I kept talking. "I just want to . . . you know. I've got fifteen dollars," I told him.

This was the weird part with me and Miller. We both hated each other, but even more than that, he wanted my money and I wanted my notebook back. Neither of us had said anything about it to Stricker, even when we both got suspended. It was like middle school Mafia or something.

Miller looked at me for a long time, like he was trying to decide what to do with me. Then he let go of my shirt.

"All right," he said. "Third-floor bathroom, five minutes."

"Five minutes," I said, and walked away, but my heart was still going just as fast as before. This was only half over.

Was it five minutes until I pulled this off?

Or five minutes to live?

CHAPTER 56

TEN PAGES AND A LIE

DON'T GO IN THAT BATHROOM!

Is that what you're thinking right now? I know, I know—what kind of idiot would let himself get cornered like that? I guess the answer is, a desperate one.

I went straight up to the third floor and waited in the hall to make sure Miller came alone. When he got there, I followed him inside, and we both checked the stalls before either of us said anything. Then Miller turned on me and held out his hand.

"Money," he said.

As soon as I gave it to him, he grabbed me and twisted my arm around behind my back.

"You think I'm stupid?" he said. He pulled that crumpled flyer out of his pocket and tried to shove it in my mouth. "You are so dead for this."

"I told you, I didn't do it!" I said, turning my head away. My arm hurt, but nothing was broken—yet.

"Don't give me that. You draw all the time. It's all over that stupid little notebook of yours," he said.

"Did you *look* at my pictures?" I said. "They aren't anything like the, uh . . . the other thing." It seemed like a bad idea to actually say "Miller the Killer Chicken" out loud right now.

"You could have faked it," Miller said. He twisted my arm some more, and I tried not to yell out. "You could have drawn different, or whatever."

"Miller, seriously!" I said. "I've spent half the year trying to get my stuff back from you. Do you really think I'd blow it on something as stupid as this?"

I was still more scared than anything, but I have to say—that was just about the most genius moment of my life. Not only did Miller buy it and finally let me go, but he gave me the ten pages I'd paid for too. Besides my arm, which hurt like crazy, I hadn't felt this good in a long time.

"How many more pages to go?" I asked him. He'd stopped giving them back to me in order, and I was losing track.

"Just keep bringing the money, and you'll find out," he said. "I'll tell you this much, though. You figure out who made these"—he threw the flyer in the garbage and then kicked the garbage can over—"and I'll give you ten pages for free."

"That's a deal," I said, and got out of there while I still could.

When I left that bathroom all in one piece, I decided Leo had to give me some major points for this after all. I'm not sure if I broke any rules that day, but it didn't even matter. I'd figured out that there's more than one way to fight a war. And believe me, that's worth a lot.

INTO THE HOMESTRETCH

Then, on the last day of the third quarter, something amazing happened.

I'd been selling Zoom out of my locker, slowly but surely so I wouldn't get caught, and when I told Miller I was ready to buy some more pages, he admitted there were only nine left.

"But the price just went up again," he said. "You can have them for twenty bucks."

I didn't even care. I had twenty-seven in my pocket, anyway, and as long as Miller didn't know that, it was almost like saving seven dollars. Even better, my school year was now officially headed into the homestretch, and Miller's reign of terror was over. (Okay, Miller's reign of terror was never over, but at least he couldn't hold that stupid notebook over my head anymore.)

I decided this was a good time to start thinking seriously about my big Operation R.A.F.E. final project. The rules were that I had to get all the way through the *HVMS Code of Conduct* before I could move on to the last round, but that didn't mean I couldn't start getting ready for it in the meantime.

After school, I rode over to the Office Mart and picked out a big heavy-duty black marker. I got the kind with the chisel tip that can make thick or thin lines with the same pen. It cost $4.99, which left me just enough to buy some flaming barbecue chips on the way home.

Back in the garage, I took a roll of masking tape from Bear's workbench, a stack of old newspapers out of the recycling bin, and a can of Zoom to go with the chips. I brought it all back to my room and stuck a chair under the doorknob for maximum security, just in case.

Next, I used the tape to put a triple layer of newspaper up on my wall so the marker wouldn't soak through when I pressed down. On top of that, I put a bunch of pages from the big sketchbook

Ms. Donatello had given me, all edge to edge so it was like a giant canvas.

Now I was ready to start practicing.

Leo sat in and gave me ideas, the way he always does. "Do it like this," he'd say, and "Try that," and "Put this over there," and "Get rid of that." It sounds kind of bossy when I write it down here but, trust me, we make a good team.

The more I practiced with that marker, the better I got. And the better I got, the faster I got, which was just as important. Speed was going to be key when it came time for the real thing.

I was starting to get excited too. As far as I was concerned, the end of Operation R.A.F.E. couldn't come fast enough. I could just see it now.

"UNFORGETTABLE"
—Principal Dwight

"RAFE KHATCHADORIAN IS A CRIMINAL... AND A GENIUS!" —Ida Stricker

"HE'S A TOTAL KHATCH!"
—Jeanne Galletta

" 👍 👍 "
—Leo the Silent

CHAPTER 58

RAFE KHATCHADORIAN IS A BIG FAT IDIOT

And then I got my third-quarter grades.

It was like someone had taken all the D's and F's from my last report card and just rearranged them in different places on the new one. In other words—two months of extra tutoring and all I'd learned was a new way to spell DDFFDF.

I knew Jeanne would be dying to know how "we" did, so I actually brought my report card with me to our next tutoring session.

"Don't take it personally," I told her. "You can't fix a car if it doesn't have an engine, right?" I even knocked on my head like it was hollow, but Jeanne didn't laugh. She just sat there staring at my grades.

I tried again. "Hey, look on the bright side. One more

quarter, and we can kiss sixth grade good-bye forever."

"Well," she finally said, "I hope so."

"You hope so?" I didn't like the sound of that at all. "What's that supposed to mean?"

"I mean, you must have thought about this, right?" she said.

"Thought about what?"

"Your grades, Rafe. You can't get report cards like this all year long and then expect to sail right into seventh. They could make you take extra classes. They could make you go to summer school. Or—" Jeanne bit her lip like she didn't want to say the next part. "Or . . . they could make you do sixth grade all over again," she said, just before my head exploded into a million billion pieces.

CHAPTER 59

CHAPTER 60

STALLING FOR TIME

I got up and walked straight out of the math room.

There was no way I was going to cry about this—not in front of Jeanne.
Not in school.
Not at all.

ATTENTION! Rafe Khatchadorian does not cry. I repeat, Rafe Khatchadorian DOES NOT CRY!

But I went straight to the bathroom and locked myself in one of the stalls, just in case.

How could this happen?

I'd spent the whole school year thinking about how to survive sixth grade, and I forgot to think about the worst possible thing. It was like getting blindsided by an aircraft carrier—

AND WHAT KIND OF IDIOT DOESN'T SEE AN AIRCRAFT CARRIER COMING?

I thought seriously about walking right out of that school and not looking back. I mean, what was the point of finishing the year if I was just going to have to do it over again?

But before I could make my move, somebody started knocking on the bathroom door.

"Rafe? Are you in there?"

It was Jeanne. Unbelievable.

I didn't answer, but the door opened anyway. "I'm coming in," she said, and a second later I could see her sneakers under the stall door.

"Rafe?"

"Go away," I said.

"It's not the end of the world, you know. It's not even the end of the school year. There's still time," she said.

"For what? A brain transplant?"

"For getting your grades up."

"Easy for you to say," I told her. "You eat fractions for breakfast."

She took a step closer, and I could see her eye through the crack of the door. If I could have flushed myself right out of there, I would have done it.

"You know what my dad would say right now?" Jeanne asked.

"Yeah. 'What are you doing in the boys' bathroom?'"

"No," she said. "He'd tell you to buck up."

"Buck up?" I said.

"That's what he always says when he thinks I'm feeling sorry for myself. 'Don't give up—buck up.'"

I got to my feet and opened the stall door. "I'm not feeling sorry for myself," I said, which was at least a little pathetic, since I was standing next to a toilet.

"Uh-huh," Jeanne said. "Could we please finish this conversation somewhere else?"

But then—*knock knock knock knock!*

Somebody else was outside the bathroom door. This was starting to get downright weird.

"Hello?" said a familiar voice. The door swung open, and Mrs. Stricker was standing there, looking ready to kill. "Rafe Khatchadorian and Jeanne Galletta! What in heaven's name is going on in here?"

CHAPTER 61

JEANNE GALLETTA IS IN TROUBLE FOR THE FIRST TIME IN THE HISTORY OF THE UNIVERSE

If you'd told me at the beginning of the school year that Jeanne Galletta was going to get sent to the office for anything besides collecting awards or being perfect, I would have laughed in your face.

And if you'd told me it was going to be for getting caught in the boys' bathroom alone with me, I would have laughed in your face, but from a safe distance because you were obviously a dangerous and insane person.

But there we were, five minutes later, sitting on that bench of shame outside Stricker's office, waiting to get yelled at.

"I can't believe this is happening," Jeanne whispered. "This is so totally unfair."

"No talking!" Mrs. Harper said from the secretary's desk.

Jeanne just shook her head. I couldn't tell if she wanted to yell, or cry, or both. So when Mrs. Harper looked away, I wrote a quick note on an old tardy slip and passed it to her.

She actually smiled when she read it, but that didn't last long. Mrs. Stricker opened her door about two seconds later and told us to come inside.

"Now, can one of you please explain this little stunt to me?" she said. "Jeanne?"

"It wasn't a stunt, Mrs. Stricker," Jeanne said, talking really fast. "It wasn't anything. I swear. We were just tutoring, and—"

"Tutoring?" Stricker said. "In the boys' bathroom?"

"It's not her fault," I said. "I went in there first, and I wouldn't come out."

Stricker just looked at me like I was speaking Russian, and then she looked back at Jeanne like she was supposed to translate.

"The point is," Jeanne said, "nobody got hurt and nothing really happened. I mean, it's not like any rules got broken. Not really."

"A very important rule was broken the moment you went into that restroom," Mrs. Stricker said. "I'm afraid after-school detention is mandatory in this case."

"*What?*" Jeanne said.

"Come on!" I practically yelled. "That's totally unfair!"

"Watch your tone, Mr. Khatchadorian. You could just as easily wind up in that detention with Ms. Galletta," Stricker said.

It took me a second to catch her drift. Jeanne and I looked at each other at the exact same time.

"Hang on," I said. "You're giving her detention and not me?"

Stricker shrugged. "Rafe, I don't think for a moment that you're blameless in all of this," she said. "But the fact is, it's not against the rules for a boy to be in the boys' bathroom. I'm sorry, Jeanne, but my hands are tied."

Then the fifth-period bell rang, and Stricker stood up. This conversation was over. She even took us out to the hall, to make sure we'd go straight to class.

Jeanne and I walked away like a couple of zombies.

"I'm really sorry about this," I told her.

"It's not your fault," she said.

"But it kind of is," I said. "If I hadn't gone into that bathroom in the first place, this never would have happened."

"Well, there's nothing we can do about it now,"

Jeanne said—but again, I wasn't so sure.

In fact, I could think of at least one thing I could do.

I looked back to make sure Stricker was still there in the hall, and waved my arms to get her attention.

"Hey, Sergeant Stricker!"

"What are you doing?" Jeanne said, but I ignored her.

"Hide-and-seek! You're it!" I yelled, as loudly as I could, and then ran straight for the nearest girls' bathroom.

CHAPTER 62

GAME OVER

So I got that detention to go along with Jeanne's, but guess what? It didn't make any difference.

Once I thought about it some more, I realized I could have gotten a hundred detentions and it wouldn't change the fact that Jeanne had gotten hers—all because of me.

Bottom line? I'd broken my own No-Hurt Rule, big-time, and I didn't need Leo to tell me what that meant: I'd just lost my third and final life in Operation R.A.F.E. The game was over. As far as the mission was concerned, I was now officially dead.

So not only was I flunking out of middle school, and not only had I hurt everyone who'd been nice to me along the way, but I'd also just crashed and burned—*in my very own game.*

End of story, right? Rafe Khatchadorian equals total loser. Nothing more to tell.

CHAPTER 63

SOMETHING ELSE

Except—you're not stupid. There are obviously still some pages left in this book. It's like when the guy in the movie goes off a cliff, and you're supposed to think he's dead, but you also know it can't be over yet. Something else still has to happen.

And something else did, but I'm going to let Leo tell that part.

CHAPTER 64

THOU SHALT (NOT) VANDALIZE

The next morning, I left a note for Mom saying that I had to go to school extra early to work on a project, which was basically true. I just left out the part about how *early* meant four in the morning and *project* meant highly illegal activity.

"You're not going to regret this," Leo kept telling me. The way he saw it, the whole point of Operation R.A.F.E. was about breaking rules, so why should I let a little thing like losing the game stop me from doing the part I'd been looking forward to the most?

Like I said before—genius.

When I got to school, I rode around behind the gym and parked my bike. There's a big empty wall back there, where we play dodgeball when Mr. Lattimore doesn't feel like torturing us himself. Before all of this, I would have just seen a wall. Now I saw a giant canvas.

I unpacked my new fat black marker, a big old camping flashlight, and some of my latest practice sketches. I'd drawn these ones on graph paper, which is kind of like a brick wall, to show me how big everything would need to be.

But Leo was feeling impatient. "You don't need those anymore," he said. "The clock's ticking. Stop thinking so much and just go."

So I did. I set up the flashlight on a rock so that it was shining right at the wall. Then I picked up my marker and started.

It was kind of slow-moving at the beginning. I wasn't sure what to draw first, or what order to do things in. But the more I kept going, the more I got into it, and then somewhere along the way everything started to flow.

"That's it," Leo said. "Put some more of that over there" and "Make this bigger" and "Try it like this" and "No—bigger. BIGGER!"

He said that a lot. After a while I was running

around like crazy, working over here, working
over there, and getting up on an old trash can
to reach the higher parts when I needed to. The
whole thing started to get so big that I felt like
I was *inside* it, even while I was still drawing.
It was like Leo had said—I wasn't thinking
anymore. I was just *doing* it, like the marker was
just another part of me, and the lines and shapes
and pictures were coming right out of my hand.
It was an amazing feeling.

I totally lost track of time too. All of a sudden,
the sun was coming up, and I was putting my
finishing touches on everything. My arm was so
tired that it felt like it was ready to fall off, but
my brain was still buzzing like crazy. I felt like I'd
never go to sleep again in my life.

In fact, I was so into it, I never even heard the
police car coming.

It pulled around the corner of the school, and
the red and blue flashers came on right away. The
car stopped short. Doors opened on both sides, and
not one but *two* policemen got out.

I froze. I didn't know if I was supposed to drop
my pen, put my hands up, or what.

But the police weren't even looking at me. They were both just standing there now, staring at my wall.

"Holy smokes, kid," one of them said. "Did you really do all this?"

CHAPTER 65

TWO MINUTES LATER . . .

CHAPTER 66

TIME OUT (AGAIN)

Did you notice something there? Just me and Leo in the back of that police car?

Way back at the beginning of this book, I showed you a picture of me, Leo, *and Georgia* in a Hills Village Police Department cruiser, and I said we'd get back to that part.

No, I'm not messing with you. Yes, that part's still coming. We just haven't gotten there yet.

Let me put it this way: Everything that happened that morning, with the mural and getting arrested, was just the beginning of the best *and* worst day of my life, all in one. There's still plenty more to tell.

So stick with me.

CHAPTER 67

HOUSE ARREST

As long as I'm at it, here's a pop quiz to see if you've been paying attention:

What do you suppose Bear did when the Hills Village Police brought me home just after sunrise that morning?

1. He bribed the cops to go away and forget this ever happened.

2. He took me out for a delicious breakfast.

3. He went ballistic and started chasing me all over the house until I locked myself in the bathroom and Mom told him to calm down or she was going to call the police back herself.

Answer: Let's just say it's a good thing I'm fast on my feet.

I stayed away from Bear after that, which

wasn't hard, since Mom sent me to my room "until further notice." It was kind of like getting an in-school suspension, without the school. I just sat there on my bed for hours, wishing I were somewhere else.

Or some*one* else. Like maybe someone who wasn't a full-time disappointment to his own mother.

"You've got to focus on the positive," Leo told me. "That was a major masterpiece you pulled off today. Nobody's going to forget this one."

"Yeah, including Mr. Dwight and Mrs. Stricker," I said. "They're probably going to kick me out of school."

A day earlier I might have even thought that was a good thing. Now all I knew for sure was that I didn't want to feel this way anymore—like no matter what I did, good or bad, and no matter how hard I tried, I just ended up back in the same place. Maybe Mrs. Stricker was right. Maybe I really was headed for the federal penitentiary someday—the ultimate detention.

Around lunchtime, Mom came back in to talk to me.

"I went to the school," she said, "and I told Mr. Dwight you'll be painting over that mural this weekend. It's a shame, really. Anywhere else and I would have been impressed."

"Are they going to kick me out?" I asked.

Mom sighed. She seemed really sad—because of me, of course. Again.

"I don't know," she said. "We have a conference at school first thing tomorrow morning. Until then you're staying right here."

As she started to leave the room, I told Mom I was really sorry, but all she said was, "I know you are, Rafe." And then she closed the door.

The only other person I saw that afternoon was Georgia. She brought me a pudding cup when she got home from school, but I think that was just so I'd tell her what had happened.

I didn't yell at her, but I did tell her to get out and stay out. I just wanted to be alone with my thoughts.

For the rest of the day it was quiet. Nothing else happened until just after dark. I heard the TV come on in the living room, and I could smell

What did YOU DO?!
Are you in BIG trouble?
Why did Mom keep you home from school?
Can I have your room?

onions cooking from the kitchen. That's when the doorbell rang, and everything went from really, really bad . . .

. . . to really, really worse.

CHAPTER 68

THE VERY WORST PART

I stuck my head out into the hall to listen.

"I've got it," Mom said.

The front door opened, but then nothing happened.

"That's weird," Mom said. "There's no one here— oh, wait. What's this?"

I heard Bear grunt the way he does when he rolls off the couch.

"What've you got there?" he said a second later. They were out on the porch now.

"I'm not sure," Mom said. Her voice was all faraway, like she was thinking about something else. I heard papers rustling.

"Not sure?" Bear said. He was getting crabby all over again. "Just look at this stuff! I'm telling you, that kid's nothing but a little hoodlum."

"Don't talk about him that way," Mom said, "and lower your voice."

"Are you kidding me?" Bear said. "Listen, if you're not going to do something about this, I will. In fact, I'm going to get him right now."

"No, you're not. Not like this," Mom said.

The front door slammed, and they started arguing outside. I couldn't understand what they were saying anymore, but it was obviously about me. My blood started to pump.

The next thing I heard was Bear roaring. "DON'T TELL ME WHAT TO DO!"

Then Mom said something I couldn't hear.

Then, "SHUT UP, JULES! JUST SHUT UP!"

I heard Mom yell, and then it got quiet—but not in a good way. I started running down the hall, and as soon as I did, I practically slammed into Georgia coming the other way. She looked really scared, and she was crying too.

"Rafe! Come help Mom, quick!"

CHAPTER 69

THE FAMOUS POLICE CAR INCIDENT

As soon as I saw that Mom had fallen down the front steps, I told Georgia to call 911.

"But—"

"*NOW*," I told her, and closed the front door behind me when I went outside.

Bear was standing next to Mom, trying to help her up, but she wouldn't let him.

"Just get away from me!" Mom was saying.

"Jules, I'm sorry. It was an accident. It was just an accident—"

"I know that," Mom said. "And I don't care. Just back off, Carl!"

It wasn't until then that I noticed all the pages, and the big envelope with MRS. K. written on

the front. They were scattered all over the porch, like somebody had dropped them there. And they weren't just any pages either. I recognized the handwriting, the drawings, all of it. They were photocopies of my Operation R.A.F.E. notebook— including a copy of every page I'd ever bought back from Miller, as far as I could tell.

But I had bigger problems to deal with right now.

I jumped off the porch and pushed Bear away from Mom as hard as I could.

"Get out of here!" I yelled at him. His mouth was hanging open, and his eyes were kind of blank, like he wasn't even there. I'd never seen him like that before. He just backed away without a fight and stood in the driveway, not leaving, but not coming any closer either.

"It's okay," Mom told me when I went to help her up. "It was just a push. He didn't mean to hurt me."

Still, I stayed right there until the police came, with two cruisers and an ambulance. They put Bear in the back of one car. Another policeman started asking me and Georgia questions about what we'd seen, while the ambulance guys looked at Mom's wrist. Georgia was crying the whole time, and I held on to her hand, which, believe me, is not something I usually do. The whole scene was crazy. It was totally insane!

"I'm okay," I kept hearing Mom say. "I'm fine." Still, they wanted to take her to the hospital for some X-rays, so she got into the back of the ambulance while Georgia and I watched. We weren't allowed to ride along, but the policeman said he'd take us.

"I'll see you there," Mom called out.

"We'll be right behind you," the policeman told her.

"And I'm right here too," Leo whispered, which was kind of a big deal for him, since he hardly ever talks when other people are around. But I appreciated it.

And by the way, if you're still wondering:

TWO TIMES IN ONE DAY! What are the odds?

CHAPTER 70

M♥M

Mom was okay. They put an Ace bandage on her at the hospital and then called a taxi for us to get home again. She sat in the back with her arms around us the whole way, even with her hurt wrist and everything.

When we got home, the first thing I saw was that someone had put all those pages back into the envelope and left it on the porch. I wasn't too happy about it, but Mom didn't say anything. She just took the envelope into the house with her, and I didn't see it again after that.

Inside, there were a couple of messages from Bear on the machine, saying how sorry he was, and thank you for not pressing charges, and how he was going to be staying at a buddy's house for the time being.

"Jules, call me," he said. "Here's the number. Five-two-four—"

Mom hit the ERASE button before he could even finish. It made me want to cheer.

"Come sit," Mom told us. "I want to have a talk."

So we all sat down at the kitchen table, with one empty chair where Bear usually ate.

"Things are going to change around here," Mom said. "Bear's not going to be living with us anymore, and hopefully that means I can afford to stop working double shifts at the diner too."

Now we did cheer. This was the best news I'd heard in forever.

But, of course, the cheering didn't last long.

"As for you, Rafe," Mom said, "there's still a lot we have to deal with."

"I know," I said. "And Mom? I'm really sorry." It felt like I'd been saying that a lot lately. Too much, in fact. Mom reached over and put a hand on my shoulder, but seeing that bandage on her wrist just made me feel worse. "What happened tonight . . . this was all my fault. I just . . . I, um—"

I didn't even know I was about to start crying. It just kind of started on its own. All of a sudden, there were tears coming out of my eyes, and my face was all scrunched up, and I was bawling like a baby. The weirdest part was that I wasn't even embarrassed. Not even with Georgia sitting there gawking at me.

"This wasn't your fault," Mom said. "Not even close."

"I'll bet you wish you could just have a normal kid sometimes," I said, wiping my nose on the paper towel she gave me.

"I'm normal!" Georgia said.

"That's not how I think about it," Mom said. "It's true, Rafe, you've made some bad choices for too long now. But I've made some bad choices too, haven't I?"

I knew she meant Bear, but I didn't say anything.

"In any case, we'll worry about all this in the morning, okay?" Mom said. Then she leaned over to whisper in my ear. "And I think normal's a little boring, don't you?"

"Hey, no whispering!" Georgia whined.

"That's what Leo says," I whispered back, and Mom smiled a kind of happy-sad smile.

"Where do you think he got it?" she said.

"Where *who* got it?" Georgia said. "Got what? What are we talking about?"

And even though I knew Leo wasn't *actually* there and that he couldn't *really* give me a thumbs-up from across the table, that's exactly what he did, anyway.

CHAPTER 71

IT HAD TO HAPPEN SOMETIME

When Mom brought me to school the next morning, everyone—and I mean everyone—was staring. I guess that meant they'd all seen my mural, which I guess was a good thing, since it was going to be gone by that weekend. A lot of people were whispering and pointing, and one guy even took a picture, but nobody said a single word to me.

With one exception.

Miller was leaning against the trophy case, watching when I came in. He had that same stupid smile on his face as always, like a giant baby who just made a good poop in his diaper.

"Hey, Khatchadorian!" he yelled over. "You get my package?"

Now, believe it or not, I'd almost forgotten about that envelope. I'd spent the whole night blaming myself for what had happened. I hadn't stopped to remember how it all had kicked off with that ring of the doorbell—just before Mom and Bear started arguing . . .

. . . and Georgia couldn't stop crying . . .

. . . and Mom ended up at the hospital.

I pulled away from Mom and ran right at Miller, just like the last time, except now we were face-to-face. I didn't even slow down until my fist plowed into his gut at full speed.

Miller looked totally shocked, but that didn't stop him from swinging back and smashing me in the nose. I felt the blood almost right away. I started to go down, but I grabbed on and twisted him around until we were both on the floor, rolling and throwing punches wherever we could. He nailed me, hard, in the stomach. I got him, kind of, in the eye—

Then Mr. Dwight was hauling us off each other, and Mom was pulling me away from Miller. We were both still yelling and screaming—I don't even remember what I said, but I probably couldn't put it in this book, anyway. My shirt was ripped down the front, I felt like I was going to throw up, and I was still bleeding.

But I couldn't help noticing that I was also still alive. I was in bigger trouble than ever now, if that was even possible, but I'd just survived Miller, kind of the way I'd survived most of sixth grade—a little beat up (okay, a lot beat up) and not exactly a winner, *but still standing*. That's more than anyone in the whole school probably would have expected from me. Including me.

So I'll take it.

CHAPTER 72

THE BIG E

Well, if it wasn't settled already, it is now," Mr. Dwight told us. "Rafe, you're being expelled from Hills Village Middle School for the rest of the year."

I wasn't too surprised but, still, I couldn't even look at Mom. She probably wanted to finish what Miller had started and kill me right now.

We were sitting in Mr. Dwight's office, along with Mrs. Stricker. I had an ice pack on my nose and a safety pin to keep my shirt closed. I felt kind of numb, in more than one way.

"Rafe can continue to get his assignments and work on them at home," Mr. Dwight was telling Mom. "And, of course, you can reenroll him in sixth grade in the fall."

It just kept getting worse . . . and worse. . . .

Then Mr. Dwight's phone buzzed. He picked it up.

"Yes?" he said, and then, "Tell her we're in a parent meeting."

But a second later, the door opened anyway, and Ms. Donatello was there.

"I'll make it quick," she said. "I understand this is a private conference, but I'd like to offer one suggestion on Rafe's behalf, if it's all right."

Everyone looked at Mom now, including me.

"Please do," Mom said, and Donatello came in.

"I was going to bring this up later in the quarter, but now seems to be the time," she said. She put a brochure on Mr. Dwight's desk where everyone could see it.

Dwight and Stricker didn't say anything. Mom picked up the brochure.

"Airbrook could be a perfect environment for Rafe," Donatello said, and then she looked right at me. "You'd have to take a longer bus ride, but I think you might like it there. The school is a combination of visual arts and academics, for nontraditional learners."

"What, like special ed?" I said.

"No," Donatello said. "It's a school for artists."

Now I started to get interested.

"Excuse me," Mrs. Stricker said. "Rafe is being expelled. Are you suggesting he should be *rewarded* for his behavior?"

"Not at all," Donatello said. "But I am saying that Rafe has talent. I've seen it all year long."

That was a first. I can't remember anyone using the words *Rafe* and *talent* in the same sentence before.

"What about his grades?" Mom said. I was looking over her shoulder at the brochure, and there were pictures of kids standing at easels and making sculptures and some stuff I didn't even know what it was.

"There's no question we'd have to work a bit on the academics," Donatello said. "But again, Airbrook is for students at all levels. If Rafe's portfolio shows promise, we might even be able to get him a needs-based scholarship."

"Portfolio?" I said.

"A collection of your artwork," Donatello said. "So they can evaluate your potential."

I was getting more excited by the second. Right now, things were looking

better than I'd ever thought they could.

That is, until Mom opened her purse, reached inside, and took out Miller's little gift package from the day before.

"I wasn't sure if I needed to bring this up or not," Mom said. "But I think now maybe I should."

That's when I knew it was all over for me.

CHAPTER 73

MOM ISN'T FINISHED

A minute later, the copies of my notebook were spread all over Mr. Dwight's desk. It was all right there—the rules for Operation R.A.F.E., every school regulation I'd broken, and all those stupid pictures Leo and I had drawn along the way. Now everyone could see exactly how much of a juvenile delinquent I was. I just stared at the floor.

"Well, this explains a thing or two," Mrs. Stricker said, and I could feel that art school slipping right through my fingers.

"Actually," Mom said, "that's not really my point."

I looked up.

"Yes," Donatello said. "I see where you're going with this. We've got the beginnings of a portfolio right here. Rafe, some of these sketches are just so *you*."

Say what?

I wasn't even sure what Donatello meant, but it seemed like a good thing.

"Mrs. Khatchadorian," Mr. Dwight said, "you're obviously welcome to enroll Rafe wherever you like, but it's important that he understands the gravity of his actions here."

"I couldn't agree more," Mom said. "And believe me, there are going to be consequences."

I could hardly stand it anymore. Where was this thing going to land?

"But you see, I've always known that Rafe is an artist at heart," Mom said. "It's in his blood. In fact, he's named for the great Rafael Sanzio of Urbino. I named all of my children after artists I admire. Rafe's sister is named for Georgia O'Keeffe."

"Nice choices," Donatello said, smiling.

"And," Mom said, "Rafe also had a twin brother."

Now I just wanted her to stop talking, but of course she didn't. She kept going.

"His name was Leonardo," she said.

"For Leonardo da Vinci?" Donatello asked.

"That's right. Unfortunately, Leo died very young," Mom said. "He got sick with meningitis when the boys were just three, and we lost him."

Donatello put a hand on Mom's shoulder. Mr. Dwight and Mrs. Stricker looked like they didn't know what to say.

"It was a long time ago," Mom said, looking at me now. "But even so, Leo's still with us in spirit. Isn't that right, Rafe?"

I just nodded. It was true, after all.

And I guess I owe you an explanation.

CHAPTER 74

AN EXPLANATION

You're probably thinking HANG ON A SECOND—all these chapters, and all these pages, and he's just now getting around to telling me that this Leo guy was actually his brother?

And I guess the short answer is—yes, that's what I'm telling you. And no, I'm not crazy. I'm okay. Really. Maybe I shouldn't have mentioned it at all, but I figured if you've stuck with me this far, you deserve to know the whole truth.

I don't remember that much from when Leo was around. His hair was lighter than mine, and he was—let's face it—kind of pudgy. In all the old pictures, it's like there's one and a half of him next to one of me. But we were both pretty little when he died. I just remember it got really quiet around the house, and my grandmother came to stay with us.

Then somewhere along the way, I started imagining what it would be like if Leo was still around. And it just kept going from there.

For the record, I'm not saying Leo's always going to be there, like he has been so far. Maybe I'll outgrow him. Or maybe I'll even find a real human best friend someday—who knows? If that happens, I'm pretty sure Leo wouldn't mind. He'll always be my brother, and that's no matter what.

In the meantime, I like things the way they are. Maybe that makes me weird. Maybe it's even part of what makes me an "artist," like Mom said, but it just kind of works for me this way. . . .

Well, except for the part about how I got into all this trouble and was about to get expelled. I know, I know—I'm working on it. Just turn the page and keep reading.

CHAPTER 75

THE BIG CATCH

Now that Mom had told Mr. Dwight and Mrs. Stricker everything there was to tell, they all kind of sat there looking at each other.

"So, anyway," Mom said, holding up the Airbrook Arts brochure, "if there's anything I can do to help make this happen, I want to do it." She put the brochure back on Mr. Dwight's desk, kind of like the ball was in his court now.

"Mrs. Khatchadorian, first of all let me say how sorry I am for your loss," Mr. Dwight said.

"We both are," Mrs. Stricker said, and she even looked like she meant it.

"Thank you," Mom said. "Now, as for Rafe—"

"May I make one more suggestion?" Ms. Donatello cut in.

Everyone looked over at her. So far, she'd been on my side, so I definitely wanted to hear what she had to say.

"Let Rafe's expulsion stand," Donatello said. "Keep him out of school for the quarter, but then let him enroll for a full schedule of classes in the summer session."

There it was—
the big catch.
Summer school!
I knew there had to be something.

"I can work with Rafe," Donatello said. "On academics as well as the portfolio, and we can see how it goes."

"Rafe?" Mr. Dwight said. "What do you have to say about all this?"

All of a sudden, everyone was looking at me, and nobody else was talking. Here was my chance to say something smart.

"I don't want to go to summer school," I said.

"WHAT?" Mom said.

Mrs. Stricker smiled a little.

Donatello looked like she'd just been totally shot down.

"But I'll do it," I said, right to Mr. Dwight. "If you'll let me."

He and Mrs. Stricker kept looking at each other. I wasn't sure if I'd convinced them, but then I thought of one more thing to say.

"Maybe I could do a real mural too," I said. "With paint and everything. Something for the school, like, to say I'm sorry."

"Actually," Ms. Donatello said, "a project like that could make an excellent part of the application to Airbrook." She looked over at Dwight and Stricker.

"That is, if we move ahead with this, of course."

At first, nobody else said anything. Then, finally, Mrs. Stricker kind of shrugged, and Mr. Dwight spoke up.

"It would have to be something appropriate. We'd need to see sketches before any paint goes on any walls."

"No problem," I said.

"And none of this can start until the summer session," Dwight said.

"And even then," Stricker said, "if we see any kind of behavioral issues—"

"You won't," Mom said, squeezing my hand. "Right, Rafe?"

"Right," I said, and tried to smile like I meant it.

Actually, I had no idea if I could pull this off. Not the mural, not the classes, not even my "behavior." But it was worth a shot if it meant trading Hills Village in for art school—*art school!*—in the fall. Maybe even as a seventh grader.

Besides, if nothing else, I figured I owed it to Mom—and to Leo the Silent, and Donatello the Dragon Lady, and yes, even Jeanne Galletta—to at least try this crazy plan.

CHAPTER 76

WHAT HAPPENED NEXT

So that pretty much brings us up to the present. I'm still expelled. The school year's not over yet. And believe me, it's no more fun being out of school than it was being in school. Mom made sure of that.

But first, let me tell you the good parts.

About a week after all this happened, Bear came to the house while Mom was at work and got his stuff. He's officially moved out now. He even forgot his own secret stash of Zoom, which I've moved to a new hiding place that I'm not even going to tell *you* about.

Meanwhile, Mom just works breakfast and lunch at the diner, so she's home every night. She's been making dinner for us ever since, and she's a *way* better cook than me, Georgia, and Bear combined.

Also, after I got expelled, Jeanne Galletta actually called me at home to make sure I was okay. I told her I was fine, but I didn't know if I was going to be back at Hills Village in the fall. Then she said, well, maybe we should go see a movie this summer, my treat, and I told her I'd think about it. (Okay, you can probably figure out which part of that isn't true, but it can't hurt to dream, right?)

And now for the not-so-good stuff.

Mom doesn't let me stay home alone, so every school day for the last six weeks, I've been coming here to Swifty's Diner. Swifty let us set up a folding table in the storage room, where I sit on my pickle tub and work on my school assignments (which seems crazy, since I'm expelled, but tell that to my mother).

I also spend an hour a day washing dishes, or sweeping, or cleaning up around the restaurant. Swifty calls it my "room and board," and it gets me a free lunch every day (eight dollars or less), which isn't too bad.

At first I didn't think I was going to make it.

Even with the homework and the cleaning job, there was still a lot of just sitting around, staring at the walls and waiting for summer school (boooo!) to start. I'd never been so bored in my life.

But then I got another idea. One of my big ones, like Operation R.A.F.E. Except, this mission wasn't a game. It was more like a special project to help me pass the time.

And guess what?

You just finished reading it.

EXCLUSIVE BONUS!

An interview with Griffin Gluck, star of the movie

MIDDLE SCHOOL
THE WORST YEARS OF MY LIFE

It's like I'm looking in a mirror.

Griffin Gluck in Middle School, to be released by CBS Films and Lionsgate. © 2016 CBS Films Inc. and JBP Business, LLC. (Photo credit: Frank Masi)

Q: HAD YOU READ THE MIDDLE SCHOOL SERIES BEFORE YOU WERE CAST IN THE FILM?

A: Yes, my friends and I read the books when they came out.

Q: WHAT WAS YOUR AUDITION FOR *MIDDLE SCHOOL* LIKE?

A: It was a long and suspenseful process. I really wanted the role of Rafe and was so happy to hear I got it!

Q: HAVE YOU ALWAYS WANTED TO ACT?

A: Yeah, I love acting! I've been acting since I was seven years old.

Q: HOW DO YOU BALANCE ACTING AND SCHOOL? WHAT'S YOUR FAVORITE SUBJECT?

A: I work as hard as I can to make sure I always have a balanced schedule between the two. My favorite subject is science.

Q: RAFE KHATCHADORIAN HATCHES A PLAN TO BREAK EVERY RULE IN THE SCHOOL'S CODE OF CONDUCT. HAVE YOU EVER BROKEN THE RULES?

A: I may have chewed gum a few times in class, but I try to follow the rules because I hate getting in trouble!

Q: DO YOU HAVE ANY SIBLINGS? IF SO, DO YOU RELATE TO RAFE AND GEORGIA'S RELATIONSHIP?

A: Yes, I have a sister who is three years older than me. She is a lot like Georgia with her clever comebacks and sometimes her snooty comments. The only difference is in their ages. My sister and I are really close and we tease each other a lot.

Q: BESIDES RAFE, WHO'S YOUR FAVORITE *MIDDLE SCHOOL* CHARACTER?

A: My brother, Leo, who is played by my good friend Thomas Barbusca.

Q: WHICH IS YOUR FAVORITE BOOK IN THE MIDDLE SCHOOL SERIES?

A: The first book, because it was the one that drew me into the series.

Q: WHICH SCENE FROM THE BOOK WERE YOU MOST EXCITED TO ACT OUT?

A: I think all of the pranking scenes were my favorite ones to act out, because I could never do that in real life.

Q: WHAT WAS IT LIKE WORKING WITH FAMOUS COMEDIANS LIKE ANDY DALY AND ROB RIGGLE?

A: It was amazing to work with them. I love

everything I see them in, and they made me laugh constantly.

Q: WHAT WAS YOUR FAVORITE MOMENT FROM FILMING THE MOVIE?

A: A lot of my best memories come from improvising lines with the whole cast while they made me crack up.

Q: WHAT DO YOU LIKE TO DO WHEN YOU'RE NOT ACTING?

A: I like to hang out with my friends, play video games, and skateboard.

Q: WHAT ADVICE DO YOU HAVE FOR YOUNG PEOPLE WHO WANT TO BECOME ACTORS?

A: Never give up. Work for what you want and stay positive.

Q: DO YOU WANT TO CONTINUE MAKING MOVIES IN THE FUTURE?

A: Yes, I hope to keep entertaining as many people as I can.

Q: ANY DREAM ROLES? WHAT ELSE WOULD YOU LIKE TO PURSUE?

A: Playing Rafe was a dream role for me, and I would love to see what's in store for him. I can't wait to see where my acting career takes me!

CONGRATS!

YOU JUST SURVIVED THE WORST YEAR OF YOUR LIFE.

ME TOO.

BUT GUESS WHAT?

HERE COMES

BUCKLE YOUR SEAT BELT.   —RK

SEE THE NEXT PAGE FOR A SNEAK PREVIEW

WHOOM!

Well, who'd have thought so much could change in one summer? Not me, that's for sure. Not my best buddy, Leonardo the Silent.

Probably not the folks at Airbrook Arts Community School either. That's where I was supposed to start seventh grade in the fall.

Supposed to. You caught that, right? There's a reason my last book was called *Middle School, The Worst Years of My Life*. Sixth grade was only the start. I've got a whole lot more to tell you about. But first I should introduce myself.

Anyway, I guess I should have seen it coming. It's like every time things start to look okay in my crazy life, something always comes along to change it. It's like it just falls out of the sky.

And *everything* changed on the day Swifty's Diner burned to the ground.

Here's what happened. See, there's this thing called a grease trap over the grill at the diner, where Swifty (also known as Fred) cooked about fifteen dozen greasy burgers every day. If you don't clean out the trap once in a while, it turns into a giant fireball, just waiting to go off.

And guess what?

I didn't get to see much. I was in the storage room in the back, just passing the time and waiting for Mom to finish her lunch shift. Then all of a sudden, I heard this giant *WHOOM!* People started yelling, the fire alarm started blaring, and I could smell smoke.

A second later, Mom was there.

"Come on, Rafe," she said. "We have to go—right now!" And she hustled me out the back door.

Anybody smell smoke?

Nobody was hurt, but flames were coming through the windows and up through the roof before the Hills Village Fire Department even got there.

By the time the firefighters finally put out the fire, Swifty's Diner looked more like Swifty's Big Pile of Ashes. Everything was all black and smoking, and the restaurant was just—gone.

And that's not all.

No Swifty's meant no job for Mom.

No job meant no money to pay the rent on our house.

No house meant we had to pack up all our stuff and get out.

(See what I mean about everything changing?)

The only place we could go was Grandma Dotty's. She told Mom we could come stay there as long as we wanted, which was really nice of her and everything, but the problem was, she lived in the city, about eighty miles away. In other words, way too far for me to even think about going to Airbrook anymore. Now I was going to be starting seventh grade at some big-city middle school, where kids like me get turned into chopped meat every single day.

So there you have it. Chapter 1 isn't even over, and I'm already starting a whole new life. Try to keep up if you can. This is only the very beginning, where I say—

Good-bye, Hills Village!
Good-bye, lucky breaks!
And hello, seventh grade!

Hey, everyone, it's me—Rafe K. Thanks for reading my story. My next mission is already in the works, and it's CRAZY big. Stay tuned! Until then, I'm sending you to another middle school prison to meet another tortured middle schooler who really knows how to keep a kid laughing! Everyone is talking about Jamie Grimm. He's hilarious. So if you're looking for a story that's, well, even FUNNIER than mine, look no further. . . .

One

FLOP SWEAT

THE PLANET'S FUNNIEST KID COMIC CONTEST

NO LAME Justin Bieber Jokes!

NO adults allowed!!
★ ★ ★ ★ ★ ★

NO ONE REALLY CARES WHY THE CHICKEN CROSSED THE ROAD

Have you ever done something extremely stupid like, oh, I don't know, try to make a room filled with total strangers laugh until their sides hurt?

Totally dumb, right?

Well, that's why my humble story is going to start with some pretty yucky tension—plus a little heavy-duty drama (and, hopefully, a few funnies so we don't all go nuts).

Okay, so how, exactly, did I get into this mess—up onstage at a comedy club, baking like a bag of French fries under a hot spotlight that shows off my sweat stains (including one that sort of looks like Jabba the Hutt), with about a thousand beady eyeballs drilling into me?

A very good question that you ask.

To tell you the truth, it's one *I'm* asking, too!

What am I, Jamie Grimm, doing here trying to win something called the Planet's Funniest Kid Comic Contest?

What was I thinking?

But wait. Hold on. It gets even worse.

While the whole audience stares and waits for me to say something (anything) funny, I'm up here choking.

That's right—my mind is a *total and complete blank*.

And I just said, "No, I'm Jamie Grimm."

That's the punch line. The *end* of a joke.

All it needs is whatever comes *before* the punch line. You know—all the stuff *I can't remember*.

So I sweat some more. The audience stares some more.

I don't think this is how a comedy act is supposed to go. I'm pretty sure *jokes* are usually involved. And people laughing.

"Um, hi." I finally squeak out a few words. "The other day at school, we had this substitute teacher.

Very tough. Sort of like Mrs. Darth Vader. Had the heavy breathing, the deep voice. During roll call, she said, 'Are you chewing gum, young man?' And I said, 'No, I'm Jamie Grimm.'"

I wait (for what seems like hours) and, yes, the audience kind of chuckles. It's not a huge laugh, but it's a start.

Okay. *Phew.* I can tell a joke. All is not lost. Yet. But hold on for a sec. We need to talk about something else. A major twist to my tale.

"A major twist?" you say. "Already?"

Yep. And, trust me, you weren't expecting this one.

To be totally honest, neither was I.

Two

LADIES AND GENTLEMEN...ME!

Hi.

Presenting me. Jamie Grimm. The sit-down comic.

So, can you deal with this? Some people can. Some can't. Sometimes even *I* can't deal with it (like just about every morning, when I wake up and look at myself in the mirror).

But you know what they say: "If life gives you lemons, learn how to juggle."

Or, even better, learn how to make people laugh.

So that's what I decided to do.

Seriously. I tried to teach myself how to be funny. I did a whole bunch of homework and read every joke book and joke website I could find, just so I could become a comedian and make people laugh.

I guess you could say I'm obsessed with being a stand-up comic—even though I don't exactly fit the job description.

But unlike a lot of homework (algebra, you know I'm talking about *you*), this was fun.

I got to study all the greats: Jon Stewart, Jerry Seinfeld, Kevin James, Ellen DeGeneres, Chris Rock, Steven Wright, Joan Rivers, George Carlin.

I also filled dozens of notebooks with jokes I made up myself—like my second one-liner at the comedy contest.

"Wow, what a crowd," I say, surveying the audience. "Standing room only. Good thing I brought my own chair."

It takes a second, but they laugh—right after I let them know it's okay, because *I'm* smiling, too.

This second laugh? Well, it's definitely bigger than that first chuckle. Who knows—maybe I actually have a shot at winning this thing.

So now I'm not only nervous, I'm *pumped*!

I really, really, *really* (and I mean really) want to take my best shot at becoming the Planet's Funniest Kid Comic.

Because, in a lot of ways, my whole life has been leading up to this one sweet (if sweaty) moment in the spotlight!

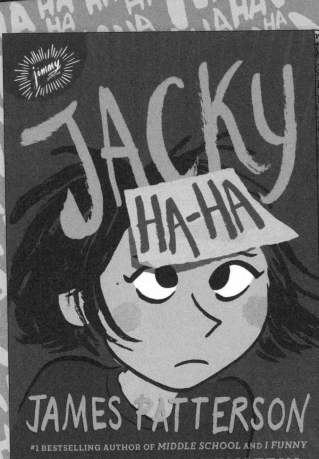

an amazing (and pretty funny) adventure!

Everyone knows that Jacky Ha-Ha is her school's biggest class clown.

BUT DID YOU KNOW SHE WAS ALSO:

REJECTED FROM *JERSEY SHORE IDOL*

THE MEANEST CATCHER IN LITTLE LEAGUE

INVENTOR OF THE HAPPY DANCE

THE ORIGINAL "NAUGHTY LITTLE DEVIL"

STAR OF HER OWN DOG FOOD COMMERCIAL

A SUPERHERO KNOWN AS THE INCREDIBLE SULK

Want to know if any of these are actually true?

YOU GOTTA READ THE BOOK!

JAMES PATTERSON received the Literarian Award for Outstanding Service to the American Literary Community at the 2015 National Book Awards. He holds the Guinness World Record for the most #1 *New York Times* bestsellers, including *Middle School* and *I Funny,* and his books have sold more than 325 million copies worldwide. A tireless champion of the power of books and reading, Patterson has created a new children's book imprint, JIMMY Patterson, whose mission is simple: "We want every kid who finishes a JIMMY Book to say, 'PLEASE GIVE ME ANOTHER BOOK.'" He has donated more than one million books to students and soldiers and funds over four hundred Teacher Education Scholarships at twenty-four colleges and universities. He has also donated millions to independent bookstores and school libraries. Patterson will be investing his proceeds from the sales of JIMMY Patterson Books in pro-reading initiatives.

CHRIS TEBBETTS has collaborated with James Patterson on five other books in the Middle School series and *Public School Superhero,* and is also the author of The Viking, a fantasy adventure series for young readers. He lives in Vermont.

LAURA PARK is a cartoonist and the illustrator of four other books in the Middle School series and the I Funny series. She is the author of the minicomics series *Do Not Disturb My Waking Dream,* and her work has appeared in *The Best American Comics*. She lives in Chicago.